Dear Reader:

It is once again my pleasure to introduce and welcome a new member of the Strebor Books family.

I recognized N'Tyse's writing talent when I selected her short story, "Caramel Latte," for my anthology, *Missionary No More*. Now N'Tyse returns with a fascinating novel of secrets and seduction.

Discover what happens when two best friends—Denise and Nadine—own a financial firm, bonding them in a business relationship while one has an eye on the other's husband. Denise decides to allow this secretive affair to continue for three years because she also has a roving eye—on one of her firm's wealthy clients.

Follow the twists and turns of love, infidelity and drama in this intriguing tale based in Texas. N'Tyse cleverly delivers all that her name stands for: Never Tell Your Secrets.

Thanks for supporting the authors in the Strebor family and for the continuous love and support that you have shown me over the past decade. I love and appreciate each and every one of you. To find me on the web, you may also go to eroticanoir.com or Facebook / Zane Strebor.

Blessings,

Zane

Publisher
Strebor Books International
www.simonandschuster.com/streborbooks

D1004891

ZANE PRESENTS

Twisted Seduction

N'TYSE

SBI

STREBOR BOOKS

NEW YORK LONDON TORONTO SYDNEY

Strebor Books
P.O. Box 6505
Largo, MD 20792
http://www.streborbooks.com

ISBN 978-1-59309-395-2
ISBN 978-1-4516-4864-5 (ebook)
LCCN 2011938323

First Strebor Books trade paperback edition April 2012

Cover design: www.mariondesigns.com
Cover photograph: © Keith Saunders/Marion Designs

10   9   8   7   6   5   4   3   2

Manufactured in the United States of America

For information regarding special discounts for bulk purchases, please contact Simon & Schuster Special Sales at 1-866-506-1949 or business@simonandschuster.com

The Simon & Schuster Speakers Bureau can bring authors to your live event. For more information or to book an event, contact the Simon & Schuster Speakers Bureau at 1-866-248-3049 or visit our website at www.simonspeakers.com.

*Dedicated to my husband, my soul mate, my other half,
Cory Williams, and our beautiful little miracle, Zanaiah*

ACKNOWLEDGMENTS

Wow, I am finally here and what a journey it has been. I say that because there have been so many tests thrown my way. So many distractions trying to veer me off my path. But I am here, stronger than ever! My God is a wonderful God and He has never let me down. I thank Him for blessing me with such talent and a gift and for keeping me sane through the rocky times. I also couldn't have gotten this far without my wonderful family who has always supported me. My loving husband, Cory; my mama, Shirley; my sister, Satoria; brothers, Donaldten and Demarcus; aunts Brenda and Letha; great-grandmother, Vernella; cousin Tierra, and all my nieces and nephews. You all know who you are. My sister-in-law, Adowri, who is always quick to volunteer to read the rough drafts. Thank you, girl! And to all my friends who were there from day one when pen first met paper. My road dawgs way back when I was spittin' and freestylin' at open mic nights, when I was grinding it out, when I was taking it all to the studio. Quadra, Angelique, Trish, Sharmeeka, Trena, Krystal, and Donyelle, you guys were there and still are. If they only knew the half of it. Lol! Todae and April, I know God put you two in my life for a reason, and I am glad that you both are in it. April, thanks for always being there when I need a second opinion on my project, or when it's crunch time and my last-minute self is running around like a chicken with its head cut off. The days and nights you would come over to help me figure something out means so much to me. To my literary friends and mentors that have been there for me since I stepped into this industry, and those that I have met along the way, I want you all to know that I appreciate you. Your time, your advice, your guidance, your support...I thank you all for it. Torrian Ferguson, Richard Carter, Brian Smith, Miasha, Joan Burke Stanford, Mark Harris, Keith Saunders (Marion Designs), Mary HoneyB Morrison, Trice Hickman, Tamika Newhouse, Anna J, Brittani Williams, Tracy Brown, and Laurinda Brown. To the entire Strebor/Simon and Schuster family, I love you guys! Zane, thank you for this wonderful opportunity. I look forward to a growing relationship. Charmaine, thanks for everything you have done to get this project up and running. Also for all the emails and updates that keep us current on what's happening in the industry. Last but not least, my agent, Dr. Maxine Thompson, and my wonderful editor, Phillip Thomas Duck. You both taught me how to really push my pen. Thank you. To all my sponsors, thank you. To all the book-clubs out there who continue to support my literary endeavors, I thank you. To all my Facebook friends that take out the time to write me, I love you guys. To all the others that offered advice, critiques, or just a simple word of encouragement, I thank you. And most importantly to all my dear loving fans:

Dear Reader,

This is my love letter to you. For you have truly been an inspiration to me. Your kind words and overall honesty has kept me grounded, as well as shaped me into the writer that I have become. I appreciate the support you have given me and the time you have taken out of your busy life, just to indulge in the fantasies I create. Your dedication touches me in a place so deep not even words can express my gratitude. It is you that motivates me to keep pushing. You that remind me all things are possible. And you that I will continue to write for. My characters shine and live only through you, and for that, I will forever be grateful.

1

Three years earlier

It was so dark and windy that night. Nadine planned on leaving right after choir rehearsal and heading straight home because she had an early morning briefing with Denise, her business partner and best friend, and the rest of their staff. They were going to discuss a strategy to save the $6 million dollar portfolio they were in danger of losing to the bank.

The car alarm to Nadine's Inuit white Audi made a chirping sound when she pressed the keyless entry remote to deactivate it. Just as she got ready to open her door, Jeff Jackson, Denise's husband, appeared out of nowhere with his arm graciously extended in Nadine's direction.

"Here, let me get that for you," Jeff offered, stepping in front of Nadine before she could reach for the door handle. "Woman, you know better than to come out here all by yourself while it's this dark," he playfully chastised.

Nadine worked up a yawn. "Isn't this sacred ground?"

Jeff let out a loose chuckle. "Yeah, but I can tell you right now that doesn't mean anything to a base-head." Jeff was born and raised in the hood and wasn't afraid to face the facts. It was a cruel world and the church they attended just so happened to be located in one of the worst parts of it.

Nadine smiled at Jeff's sincere concern for her safety. She leaned over to place her purse on the passenger seat. The fruity air freshener that hung from the neck of her rearview mirror had the entire car smelling like a watermelon patch. The scent was so strong, Nadine instantly regretted choosing it over the jasmine floral deodorizer she normally bought. She slowly turned back around to face a tower of smooth and handsome dark chocolate. Jeff was well dressed as always, wearing a black, two-button, single-breasted suit jacket; underneath it a white French-fly dress shirt. Blue denim instead of dress pants. Nadine never thought a pair of jeans could look so damn good on a man. She struggled to keep her gaze from settling on Jeff's lower half, allowing her eyes to take in his large white patent leather Jordans; at least a size twelve in her estimation. Not only did Jeff have a natural swagger, he had a sense of style, too. Old school flava with New Age spunk and looks that could conjure the panties right off a woman.

Nadine's eyes hungrily examined him from head to toe. Something was missing and then it hit her at once; his glasses. With the bit of light from her car, she was able to look straight into his mesmerizing chestnut-brown eyes.

"Where's Denise?" she inquired finally. "I thought she'd be here tonight." She pushed her hair behind her ears. It never failed. Every time she found herself in Jeff's presence, she grew nervous. Out of the six years she'd known him, that butterfly feeling still swarmed around the pit of her stomach, holding her accountable for all of her woulda-coulda-shouldas.

Jeff folded his arms. "I don't know where my wife is. She said she needed to take care of some things at the office and then she'd be heading over afterwards, but"—Jeff scoffed as he looked around the empty parking lot—"I guess we can see she never got around to it. So she has me running her errands." He raised a stack of Christmas programs bound together with a thick rubber band. But even if Denise hadn't asked him to drop off the programs, he probably would have volunteered, knowing that Nadine would be here. He relished every chance to see her. He just wished that one day he could work up the nerve to tell Nadine how he'd truly felt about her all these years.

Nadine's furrowed eyebrows showed her suspicion because Denise hadn't mentioned missing rehearsal when they spoke two hours prior. Or maybe Denise had and Nadine was just too tired to remember. But had Nadine known in advance, she would have considered skipping rehearsal herself. She could barely stay awake. She glanced down at her watch, blinked sleepily.

Jeff tried not to stare at Nadine, but failed terribly. His disobedient eyes scanned her 5'8" frame. He was checking all of her out and with God as his witness, Nadine was still the finest woman he'd ever laid eyes on. "So where you heading off to?" he asked, examining her from a new angle.

Nadine's reply was uneven. "I'm headed home. It's so late." She stifled a yawn. "Excuse me. Not only is it past my bedtime, but your wife and I have an early meeting tomorrow with a client that wants us to analyze his accounts. Can you believe that after all the time we spent winning him over, he continues to make us jump through hoops and over hurdles to maintain just a piece of his portfolio?" She shook her head, allowing the frustration that had been lurking all day to show its ugly face. "All the money we made for him and now he's ready to bail out on us. Some people are so damn ungrateful—!" Nadine caught herself, raised her right hand to the sky, bit down on her tongue as a faint smile appeared. "Lord, forgive me. That was so unladylike."

Jeff shook his head, smiled. "Don't worry about it. You must have forgotten that I'm married to a woman that cusses like a sailor. Besides, if something is on your mind, let it off."

Nadine inhaled as much of the polluted night air as she could take in at once. "It's just"—she raised her hands and then dismissed the thought altogether once she felt herself getting worked up again—"Never mind."

Jeff stood directly in front of Nadine, taking in her radiant smile, sexy aura, and the beautiful personality that had first attracted him to her way back when. He often wondered what would have happened between them if he'd confessed to her early on that she was a longing desire he kept tucked in the nest of his heart. He imagined what it would have been like marrying Nadine instead of Denise. He envisioned Deandra, his daughter, having Nadine's brown, narrow eyes, round nose, and smooth butterscotch skin so enticing it was only a fraction away from appearing edible. And since the day they'd first met, he often fantasized about making love to Nadine whenever he was intimate with Denise. He imagined making memories between her legs as she counted backwards from ten, a digit for every inch of his blessings. He fantasized about stroking Nadine so deep that in the middle of her climax she'd call out his name in a cursing fit because he was fucking her so damn good. Then before she could even cross that finish line, he'd deepen his thrust, harden his stroke, grab her by the waist and force her warm erotic passion to surrender to his own as they rode the waves of ecstasy together. Jeff couldn't get Nadine out of his head and the only thing he felt guilty about was the realization he didn't want to. She supplied him with peace and didn't even know it.

"Oh! Have I lost my mind?" Nadine blurted, breaking Jeff's concentration with a smile that exposed straight white teeth shaped by childhood braces. "How could I stand here and not congratu-late you on the new promotion? I hear you're running things now, Mr. General Manager." She straightened her posture. "So when I'm out of a job tomorrow," she said, pointing a perfectly mani-cured finger at herself and then at Jeff, "I'll be running over to your job. Sell a few cars, sweep some floors, hang balloons or something." She laughed. While Nadine was only joking, the weight of her last comment forced her to lean back against her driver door. It was as though she just set off an explosive the way the words ricocheted from her mouth, leaving a terrible aftertaste. The uncomfortable thought of working for anyone other than the extremely wealthy clients who bankrolled her lifestyle was depressing, not to mention a hard pill to swallow. She could never go back to the clock-punching days that barely financed a third of her wardrobe. She could barely eat off of those checks, she remembered painfully. If it hadn't been for the aunt that raised her and put her through school, she didn't know how she would have managed.

Before allowing the threat of losing their most prized client take hold of her, Nadine switched her mindset back to the present. She sucked in her lips. *Now what were we just talking about?* she thought. Finally remembering, she said, "So I guess everybody's *hustling* nowadays to maintain what they have. This recession has really hit us in the financial industry."

Listen to her. Jeff laughed inside at how she carefully pronounced every word. Even when Nadine tried to fit in and speak the lingo, the slang, it just didn't sound right coming out of her mouth. But her attempts were always flattering. "Yeah, everybody's gotta have a back-up plan to stay on top of all this madness," he replied. "But speaking of hustling, Denise and I just got into an argument about that the other day. She thinks I'm working too much over-time, but hell, that was in my job description. She was unhappy with me *just* selling cars. Now that I'm managing the dealership, she's still unhappy."

Nadine's face showed her concern. Denise normally shared every-thing with Nadine about her marriage, but surprisingly she hadn't mentioned anything to Nadine about this. As far as Nadine knew, Denise was ecstatic about her husband being promoted to general manager; at least proud enough to share the news with the entire staff one day in a board meeting.

"Well, you guys will work it out," Nadine assured him with a questionable sincerity in her voice. She allowed herself a brief pause, then continued. "Seriously, how long have I known you two to go through these periods of being mad over nothing?" She answered for him, her neck moving with each word. "Too long. It must be a marriage thing," she said, shrugging her shoulders, at a loss for a better explanation. Before the sentence left her mouth though, Nadine knew she was lying to Jeff. She tried coaching herself on the next best thing to say until she saw the look of unhappiness swell in his eyes. What had she gotten herself into now? Jeff and Denise's marriage wasn't any business of hers, she kept telling herself, and it would only complicate things if she stood there and allowed him to express himself in a way that made Denise look like a foolish woman undeserving of a good man. Because that would open up doors. Doors she knew should remain closed.

The wind sent another invasive chill and, instantly, Nadine's nipples hardened into bullets as thick as her pinky. The swell of her breasts made the silver, buttoned-down blouse she wore dislodge itself from the waist of her pencil skirt. That should have been her cue to leave but instead she reached in her car, started the engine, and permitted the heat to circulate between them.

Jeff stared into thin air, then back at Nadine. "I just don't know sometimes." He tilted his head. "It's like whatever I do, it's just not good enough anymore," he exclaimed honestly. He couldn't figure out where he'd gone wrong in their relationship but it was apparent that Denise was so wrapped up in herself and everything else that he didn't even exist in her world. That was why it was so easy for him to put in fifty to eighty hours a week and not feel missed at home. When Denise did decide to throw the shit up in his face, it was right before they became intimate. But Jeff was no fool. He knew that it was just another lame ass excuse to keep him from bothering her for sex. So before the night was up, they would be screaming and shouting, then to the couch he would go to finish himself off alone. There was nothing about their marriage that felt special anymore; nothing that gave him a reason to come home every night or a reason to remain faithful. Everything leading up to the point he was at now had been a living hell. And while the pussy coupons women threw his way should have been the quick fix he needed, they did absolutely nothing for him. His only true interest was in one woman—Nadine Collins.

Nadine couldn't help but wonder where all Jeff's complaining was coming from. It was all so sudden, and not that she minded being a listening ear, tonight was just not a good night for it. She had no choice but to refuse to listen to his gripes about Denise, because she was already yawning and struggling to keep her eyes open, and also struggling to keep them from drifting down to the fly of his jeans. That may have actually been the bigger struggle. Oh how she wished just for one second that she had X-ray vision. She moved closer to him.

"Jeff, honey, I want you to try to relax," Nadine said in her calmest voice. She began rubbing his shoulders. He was tense, almost as tense as the muscles in her pussy. She focused on those stubborn knots, massaging her fingers deeply in and out of every groove. Before she knew it, she had gotten herself wet. She looked around the parking lot, which thankfully was now empty except for Jeff's black BMW parked in the far corner under a leaning thirty-foot elm tree. She didn't want to risk someone coming out of the church and seeing the two of them alone.

Jeff tried to loosen up under Nadine's irresistible touch. He didn't want her to feel sorry for him, or maybe he did. He wasn't sure what he wanted Nadine to feel. As long as he had her attention, he was content. "Nothing I do is good enough anymore," he went on to say. "All Denise does is nag. It's like she creates reasons to be pissed at me. And do you know how long it's been since we had sex? Y'all are girls so I know y'all talk about it." If Nadine didn't know, he was about to enlighten her. "Three months! She tell you that?" Jeff held up three stiff fingers. "Not one, not two, but three!"

Nadine stood wide-eyed and fully awake now. She had no idea all of this was happening, and right under her nose because Jeff was absolutely right; she talked to Denise about almost everything. No subject was off limits. At least that's how it used to be.

"Please, help me understand how a woman just loses the desire to be with her man," Jeff said. "Her husband." He stared at Nadine's face, studying her facial response like an open book test. "I mean, come on. Help a brother out. What is she thinking? Is she seeing somebody? You can tell me." He scratched at the coal black waves in his Caesar haircut. "I'm just not getting this shit right now."

Nadine didn't know what to do or say but she could both empathize and sympathize because she wasn't getting any loving either. She'd been celibate for what felt like a decade. Celibate after her last fling had given her crabs, had her rushing to the hospital like a damn fool for believing his two-timing ass when he told her he wasn't seeing anyone else. Since then she vowed to refrain from sex until the timing was right. She'd been so engulfed in work lately she hadn't had the time or patience to date. Besides, in her book, most men were dogs and she refused to waste the time and energy searching for Mr. Right when she had Mr. Right Quick tucked away safely in her bedside nightstand.

"Jeff, I think you really need to talk to your wife about all this.

I mean"—Nadine's eyes widened as she flipped both her hands over—"don't you think Denise is the one that needs to hear everything that you're telling *me*?" She hoped she wasn't being hypocritical by saying so.

"Nadine, Denise and I have had the talk a thousand times. It's come to the point where it's pointless with her. She ain't hearing me." He sounded like a man out on his last limb. Speaking with no certainty, hope, or faith for a future with Denise as husband and wife. He could feel the wrinkles in his forehead beginning to form naturally like they've done throughout the course of his marriage. He often wondered if they were permanent lines of love, hate, and unhappiness that would one day interfere with the man whom he had set out to be.

"Maybe I'm just asking for too much. I bet that's it. Where is the woman that doesn't mind if her man is the main breadwinner, the head of the household, the father to their children, and her lover when it's time to be?" Jeff shook his head and took a deep breath. "I guess it's silly of me to think such a woman exists. Hell, I shouldn't have to be in competition with my wife!"

Jeff's titanium wedding band shone like a knight's armor even in the darkest hour. This symbolic piece of jewelry made its statement so loud and clear that Nadine had to avert her eyes. She forced back a silent jealousy that nearly washed up the day's dinner; now a little apprehensive about carrying on the rest of their conversation. Her ears drew themselves to the sound the leaves made as they rustled across the pavement. Maybe the leaves' efforts to escape from their original habitat was Nadine's second cue to get the hell up out of here herself. But while there were so many reasons she needed to turn around and leave, there was only one that kept her standing on her feet with her heated pussy inviting itself into their conversation.

"Jeff, I really wish I could stay and talk about this with you, but,

I don't think I'm the most suitable person to give you relation-ship advice. I don't even have a man myself." She smiled, hoping the gesture would save her from continuing the chat. She didn't feel it was appropriate to discuss Denise's bedroom drama with Jeff. Something about it didn't sit well, but she couldn't deny that being in Jeff's company felt so damn good. His conversation made her moist. Tempted her in ways she didn't realize she could be tempted. Mind-fucked her thoughts so deeply she was on the verge of having a mental climax, if that were even possible.

Nadine snatched her mind out of the gutter. They were just talking. No harm in just talking, she told herself. She begged for the right words to come but they were somewhere resting in the cracks of her mental palace. They'd locked themselves up and ingested the keys. "What I mean is," she continued, "or I can only assume, that men and women go through periods where they stop..." She was silenced before she could complete her sentence. Jeff leaned in, halting her with a kiss so passionate and so intense. She lifted her hands in the air, trying with little success to avoid touching his body. Fearful that once in his embrace she wouldn't be able to let go. She began pulling away. "Jeff!" She quickly wiped her mouth, looking behind Jeff for a moving soul. From what she could see the coast was still clear.

2

*J*eff backed away slowly, shocked by his own actions more than anything. He took a look around. They were on God's property. He felt guilty a hundred times over. Swore he heard the flames of Hell whistling his name. "Nadine, I'm so sorry," he tried apologizing. "I shouldn't—" He shook his head in disgust before stopping altogether, trying to find at least an ounce of composure while leaving his apology incomplete. "Please, Nadine, Denise doesn't have to know what happened here tonight."

That quickly Nadine had almost forgotten who Denise was. She pulled her long stream of extensions to the right side of her face. A pregnant pause juggled the words that went unsaid. "I won't say anything," she rattled out. "We just can't ever let it happen again." Nadine sucked in her lip, sampling the sweetness Jeff had left on her mouth to savor long after he was gone. A part of her couldn't resist the excitement she felt. She pulled nervously at her blouse, wishing she could rip the damn thing clean off and reveal the buttercups in Victoria's Secret made to look like full moons on a dark and chilly December night. But instead, she fanned herself as if the breeze blowing over her shoulders wasn't cool enough. Every thought was without purpose at that moment because all that she was capable of really considering was how she wanted to feel Jeff again.

"Well, I guess I better get my ass on home," Jeff stated through the sudden awkwardness that engulfed them. "I've caused enough trouble for one night." He was too embarrassed to look at Nadine's face now. He could only guess all the things she must have been thinking of him.

Nadine moved forward, slowly, closer to Jeff's hard body. She refused to let him leave her this way. In this predicament. Fuck her disagreeing good-girl conscience. She placed her lips on his again and, using her hands, gradually began making a long over-due love connection. Her fingers crawled underneath Jeff's shirt, up his solid six-pack, and over the fine black hairs spread across his chest. She inhaled his masculinity, falling in love with the scent of a man she'd only dreamed of being this close to. Her hands moved upward, allowing her fingers to snake his neck, his goatee, and the trim of his mustache.

Jeff stood there motionless, refusing to stop her. He wanted what Nadine wanted, probably more so than she.

Even in her four-inch Casadei pumps, Nadine's head only reached Jeff's shoulders. She fastidiously unbuckled his belt, unzipped his jeans, and blindly reached in through the opening. She let out a stricken gasp as her fingers traveled up and down the trunk of his dick. His pubic hairs prickled her skin as he grew in the palm of her hand. Each and every artery her fingers rolled over had a heartbeat of its own.

"Oh my God," Nadine said, panting, reacting to how well endowed he was. She stroked him to a silent satisfaction, feeling his dick stretch all of its ten full inches. This was torture, but that didn't stop her at all. She wanted Jeff so damn bad that her taste buds were sweating.

Jeff dropped the church programs he'd been holding in his hand. They landed at his feet. He tangled his fingers in Nadine's hair, drowning himself in the soft floral scent that oozed from her pores. Two tiny steps backwards and he was up against her car, fighting a losing battle. He gave into the temptation as she handled him below. A stronger breeze blew right over them and violated his manhood the second his pants hit the ground. He watched Nadine's beautiful face gradually disappear until the only visual that remained of her was the top of her head. He nearly lost it when her mouth began to caress his dick, leaving him overwhelmed with newborn fantasies. "Not here. Not like this," he murmured, unable to contain himself.

Nadine used the head of his penis to trace all the features on her face, starting with her nose, her shapely thin cocoa-painted lips, and her slight doubled chin. Excitement leaked from his tip and if there were any doubts, they'd faded away. He was enjoying this as much as Nadine was. She examined his manhood one final time, thinking of the favoritism the Creator showed when He made Jeff. She eased out her tongue, curved it a little, then allowed the syrupy glaze that coated the head of his shaft to lube her throat.

"Aww shit," Jeff cried out. He couldn't watch, not even for a second. So as his dick fell into the warm oven of Nadine's mouth, he fought to not let go and make himself out to be an embarrassment. It'd been so long. So long since he'd felt a feeling as great as the one he was experiencing at that moment. He was unstable and almost at the brink of sending his children down the back of her throat when she stopped suddenly. He opened his eyes, fearing that something was wrong.

Nadine swallowed the appetizing marinade that coated the inside of her mouth. Jeff's hands were already traveling over her body, befriending her small breasts every chance they got. With her lips still wrapped around his head, she bottled as much of him as she could fit into her mouth, moaning with anticipation.

Just when Jeff thought Nadine was done, she picked up her pace, sending him back on a thrill ride down her esophagus.

The way Nadine deep-throated him, Jeff worried he'd rip out her tonsils. He let her have her way with him. This was her ball, her court. He was only a visitor, thankful enough for the playtime. "You're taking me there," he warned her. "I can't...control what happens." He had to talk his nut down to keep from exploding.

Nadine allowed Jeff to slide from between her lips as she stood readily to her feet. His mouth moved up her slim neck, planting tight kisses along the way. She was so tasty not even his wife could substitute for a taste as fulfilling.

"Fuck me. Here. Now," Nadine whined in his ear. She was so caught up in the moment that she refused to be taken lightly. She was hot, her pussy was begging for his yardage, and she needed comfort. She wanted to be sure he knew just that. She held him tightly as his head moved between her shirt, his teeth yanking off the nickel-sized buttons on her $200 blouse along the way. "Oh yes!" she squealed in delight. She held on like a horseback rider, propping one leg on the driver's seat as he tickled her nipples with his tongue. His head started to move further below and suddenly she felt a cold chill sneak up her spine. Jeff was sliding up her skirt, leaving the responsibility of keeping her warm completely to the heater as he tasted the flesh between her pasty thighs. Before she knew it, before she could get a hold of herself, his tongue was sliding up against the thin lace outlining her thong. "Oh Jeff!" she moaned.

Jeff lifted Nadine from her feet and maneuvered her body into the car. He eased her across the beige leather seats, sending everything on the passenger side flying to the floor. With the tail of her skirt hiked way above her stomach, Nadine's underwear was the only thing keeping him from going after what he longed for.

Being the determined man that he was when it came down to moments like this, he slid those cock-blockers to the side. Her freshly waxed middle greeted him as her glistening lips encouraged his dick to reconsider its position, but Jeff's tongue argued for the first sampling.

Nadine spread her legs as far apart as the tight space they were in would allow. She looked up, watching the twinkling stars through her sunroof. It all seemed surreal. She took a deep breath and felt her skin break out in chills once Jeff's lips brushed against her hairless pussy in a swift upward motion. They enveloped her so tightly.

Hungry for it, his tongue dived between her drunken lips for the third and fourth time. Nadine began to experience her nut awakening from its coma. She matched his movements, ready to be taken there.

Jeff pleased Nadine orally with dinner table manners. He wanted every ounce of what she offered and he didn't dare stop. But his dick was weighing him down, knocking him off balance. Something had to give.

When Nadine felt just the mushroom top of Jeff's hardness rise up inside of her, she knew she hadn't felt a damn thing yet. She tried to brace herself, pulling at his jacket until she heard it rip in two places.

He plunged into Nadine in short, then deeper strokes. Each thrust taking his mind further and further away from his wife and the unhappily married category of which he was a member. He could feel Nadine's waves crashing against and along the ride of his wood, escorting him on that magical tour to epiphany. It felt so good to him that he forgot everything that mattered in his life and everything that didn't. His conscience had left him to fend for himself with a heart that no longer gave a fuck. It was a dangerous combination and an unstable position to be in, but nonetheless, here he was and he'd be damned if he pulled out like a coward. Not with the beautiful song playing in her voice after each of his long strokes.

Nadine wrapped her legs tightly around Jeff's body like a cocoon, inviting as much of his company that she could accept. Their bodies rocked in a fast forward motion and she panted and heaved until her breaths came in nearly asthmatic gasps. She felt an exhilarating sensation soaring through her. Swore up and down she was seeing doubles. "Oh God," she cried out.

Jeff was in his own world. He focused his mouth once again around the dark berries of her breasts, the inspiration that persuaded him to keep fucking her.

"I'm cumming," Nadine volunteered. The happy feeling skating around her pussy prepared her for what she was only seconds away from experiencing.

Jeff let out another powerful grunt. He didn't slow down, only picked up the pace until he was moving with the puissance of a missile. He buried his large hands underneath the roundness of Nadine's ass, squeezing both of her cheeks like putty. She begged him to fuck her harder, deeper, and so he did. With every swerve Jeff took back all the years he stayed silent and ignored the possibilities that rested with him every night as he slept soundlessly next to a stranger and a woman whom he had grown to both love and hate. So the enlightening treat he received from Nadine was love and sacrifice on a two-way street.

With closed eyes, Nadine's entire body began to shake along with Jeff's. It felt like an earthquake had come to Dallas. Tears drained from the pockets of her eyes but she couldn't comprehend why.

Nothing was crystal clear for Nadine until she was back at home, washing away their sex from her skin. She thought that if she soaked in her marble garden tub long enough, submerged in her favorite Island Breeze bath salts, that Jeff's scent would leave her body. Or that maybe if she told herself enough times that they didn't have sex, she would start to believe it. She wanted to pretend she hadn't seen Jeff at all that night, and that the idea of seeing him was merely just a passing thought that never played itself out. It took everything in her to stabilize the truth, and while she never intended to hurt Denise, she knew subconsciously that was exactly what she had done. There was no way to turn back the hands of time so the only choice left was to figure out a way to make it right. Was she sorry? Hell yes. Would she let it happen again? Only time would tell.

3

he thunderous cry from the rain startled Nadine as she lay alone in a dark room, across her bed, back strapped to the sheets. She watched a dim shadow of her naked silhouette dance along four-dimensional, coffee-caramel painted walls, flickering flames its oceanic backdrop. Luther Vandross was getting his first break since the moment she popped him into her CD player, and so were the neighbors that shared her second floor.

She glanced over at the glowing red digits on the satellite box, only to be reminded how pathetic she looked and how desperate she felt the longer she laid there waiting up for her man. She couldn't believe that she had been lying in the same somnolent position for three hours straight. Besides the numbness in her ass and despite the waterworks, she was okay. This wasn't anything new to her, she kept telling herself. She had grown accustomed to the routine months ago so there was no logical reason for her to lie there in pity and pretend for one second that she didn't know what time it was. She'd established a long time ago that she was *just* the other woman. So, stripped of her complaining rights, Nadine accepted the reality of her situation. Because before things got so deep, complicated, and almost unbearable, Nadine Collins was getting exactly what she longed for.

In the beginning, Nadine and Jeff's relationship had been about old suppressed desires she'd had since college. Feelings she could never shake, regardless of how hard she tried. She had wanted Jeff the first day she laid eyes on him. She remembered having an unforgettable feeling sweep over her entire body. It was like they shared a secret connection and, as time went on, the attraction grew to the point she could barely stand to be in the same room with him. The mere smell of his cologne made her pussy throb, and the sound of his voice taunted her late at night as she lay in bed, all alone. It was torturous to say the least.

Intertwined with the lustful cravings she shared with Jeff was the added benefit of convenience. Nadine could focus on her work and her business without feeling obligated to anyone but herself. That was why her secretive arrangement with Jeff made the uncomfortable situation work perfectly. He found his way into her arms when he needed to be held at night. And it was her pussy he crawled inside when he sought the comfort of release. She was there for him unconditionally. She was his emotional pillow, his companion, and his lover. Nadine zealously volunteered for every and any position, supplying him with everything that he was missing in his own home. She knew her place in Jeff's life and she knew exactly what she was sacrificing to remain there.

That, of course, was how Nadine felt about everything in the *beginning*. Now, the uncompromising side of her wanted his wife to know that she'd been more than friends to Jeff, three of the nine years he and Denise had been married. But it was Nadine's fear of losing Jeff that would force her to check that selfishness right at the door, because the last thing she wanted to do was make the situation more difficult than it already was.

Nadine checked the time once again. It seemed that all of a sudden everyone and everything was against her getting the satisfaction she craved tonight. She grew weak and frustrated as every staggering minute turned into an hour and then hours of her wanting, needing, dying to be fucked. Still, she waited her turn, hoping that in any given moment her phone would ring.

It was now a quarter past ten and Jeff still hadn't called to say if he'd be able to slip away from wifey tonight. Nadine reminded herself to "play fair" and "not get greedy"; that she was being inconsiderate of the circumstances. But, and there was always a BUT, her body still wanted what it wanted, when it wanted it. And right now, it wanted Jeff Jackson and his stiffness between her soaking thighs, putting her out of a week-long misery. Those lonely feelings that tugged at her heart, coupled with the dying need to feel him inside of her warmth, were the reasons for her irrational thinking. She believed she owed her pussy a long explanation as to why Mommy wasn't satisfying its thirst tonight, or for the past few nights.

She tried wrapping her mind around her situation, and as always, she'd make excuses to hide from the truth. She knew undoubtedly that she was jeopardizing her lifelong friendship with Denise. She also couldn't exclude what would become of their partnership, Platinum Crest Investments, the only black-owned investment firm in Texas. It was the business they had both built fresh out of college with no office, no experience, and only one client to their name, which happened to be Nadine's Aunt Mickey. That gamble alone should have been more than enough reason to call it quits with Jeff, but it wasn't because Nadine was in too deep.

As much as she hated to admit it, all of the rules she'd established with Jeff were broken long ago. It was a blind-sided reality that she was faced with every day before climbing out of bed. At times she even referred to it as her morning wake-up call. She no longer saw Jeff as just a sex machine rollercoaster ride she could jump on and jump off of with a push of a few buttons. Hell no, this shit wasn't that simple anymore. She had crossed lines she told herself she would never cross, buried and lost her mind in the roots of false hopes and fantasies, and on top of all that, she had fallen in love. Nadine was so deeply in love with Jeff that nowadays when he came around, she didn't want him to leave. She wondered if things were flipped, if she'd be *all* that he needed instead of finding herself in the dark about another woman he kept on the side, the exact way he was doing with Denise about her.

Nadine realized how she had foolishly tricked herself into believing that their torrid affair was nothing more than an innocent circumstance. It was destiny intervening at its best. To plead her case, she was only a bystander. A well sought out victim of Cupid and his deceiving love games. The hardest part to face in this would come later, much later, as the two of them would fall, spent, into each other's arms, high off their own orgasmic overdoses. That drawn-out moment that seemed to last forever was when Nadine somehow knew their relationship would never last. It was the instant he would mouth the words, "I have to go." A moment when her heart would sink deeper into her chest, her soul would howl in outrage, and the invisible sword dicing her feelings like chopped vegetables—would leave her bleeding internally and alone to rot. But standing before him, she'd hold her stubborn ground and fight back tears of disappointment, regret, jealousy, and bitter heartache.

Nadine found herself torn between the same old thing—her settling for second best. Tonight the statement was more true than any other time she'd spoken or thought it, because sadly, while her lover was probably out treating his wife to a fancy Valentine's dinner and lavish suck-up gifts, she was unfortunately the one at home, alone, horny as hell, and needing more than a dozen pink roses and a sixty-dollar box of chocolates to satisfy her appetite.

She resorted back to feeling used, back to feeling like throwing in the towel because she couldn't get past the fact that her incredible nights of passion relied on another woman's husband.

She tried to give it a break. At least he was thoughtful enough to buy her gifts, she reasoned, glancing over at the beautiful flower arrangement that decorated the mantle over her brick fireplace. She slipped out a piece of the Godiva chocolate raspberry truffle from the gold box. She rubbed the hard piece of chocolate against her lips. Slowly inching out her tongue, she slid the truffle from the center to the tip. She closed her eyes and tried to act natural while pretending it was Jeff gliding up and down her wet tongue.

The delectable sweetness started dissolving the instant it stroked her flesh, and the warm sticky pink filling that poured from its center, dangled like silly-string from her chin before latching on to her neck. Nadine stuck her index finger inside of her mouth to saturate it. She wiped at the stickiness clinging to her neck until it vanished into her pores. She couldn't resist taking a finger and escorting it below to her crying pussy. She swept it back and forth over her budding arousal, collecting the tears that dripped endlessly. She was so wet. So needy. She then sent the lucky finger ice-skating down the hills of her terrain.

She acknowledged how swollen her lips had become and how warm and slippery they felt against her hand. Her legs separated as she eased one finger inside her love box. Just the feel of her own finger navigating its way between the rainfalls of her vagina made Nadine feel sorry for herself. It was so damn familiar and she couldn't bear lying there for a moment longer rejecting her body of its only tension relieving medicine—dick! Jeff's dick to be exact. But where was his black ass when she needed him? She stopped fingering her pussy all at once, giving and accepting her condolences in return.

It was turning out to be a lonely and dreadful night for Nadine on what felt like the worst celebrated holiday ever. But she'd made it through the day and now all she had to do was fathom the rest of the night, so for a while longer she remained stretched out on her bed, checking the clock, then the volume on her phone just in case somehow, someway, the ringer tripped itself off. She couldn't keep this up. Frustration settled back in and, in seconds, it mutated into anger. Nadine was on the verge of calling Jeff on his cell phone and going off. Even thought about driving thirty-eight miles east to her best friend's house, storming up to their bedroom, and demanding Jeff fuck her, too. Just as hard. Just as good. She paced her breathing, dismissed those ludicrous thoughts, and then painfully accepted the burdening possibility that she wouldn't be seeing him tonight.

She blindly reached for the gold silk sheets hanging off the edge of her bed. She pulled them over her exposed body and up to her neck when another shout from the rain made her eyes pop wide open. She hated when it stormed. Maybe tonight Mother Nature was teaching her a lesson. She stubbornly kicked off the covers and stared past the ten-foot vaulted ceiling for answers she already owned. She wondered if this was how Denise felt on the nights when Jeff wasn't with her. Wondered if Jeff's side of the bed felt as cold as hers did now. *Why am I doing this to myself?* she thought, certain that no pain was greater than the feeling of having her heart set on fire by the man she loved.

Surely only a woman in her shoes or one that had walked a mile or two in them would hear her when she complained, *This shit isn't fair!* Such a woman could certainly relate to how betrayed the heart feels when the only somebody you've ever cared about is already taken; how your pussy cries and aches for your man in the middle of the night; how you lose yourself inside of him and couldn't find your way out even with a GPS navigational system. These women would agree about the circumstances that allowed a man to become the center of their world. It was only those women that could identify with Nadine's agony and not judge her position in this. That self-inflicted hurt she experienced wouldn't go down without a testimony. "It's not fair," she said aloud, this time as tears began to well in her eyes.

Trampling over the same emotional arguments that never got her anywhere, Nadine drowned out the idea of leaving. She had invested way too much to give up on Jeff now, she reasoned. He was as much her husband as he was Denise's. Nadine was committed to the affair. Their intimacies were their vows, and she would never break them. Therefore, she knew to keep doing what she'd been doing for the past three years. Be patient. He'd be here.

he ache between Nadine's legs nearly numbed her entire body while the heat burning from the fireplace continued to melt the remaining box of candies beside her. The rain rumbled again, followed by the loud bang of Nadine's heavy front door closing shut. Her heart skipped a beat. She got out of the bed, swept across the octagon-shaped Persian rug. She stopped and monitored her breathing, not wanting her excitement to send her running for her asthma pump. She took her time opening the sliding glass door that segregated her bedroom space from her office and living area, knowing for certain that it could only be one person. The only person with keys to her condominium. She stopped at a support column, draping one arm around it. Her eyes stared at the figure emerging from behind. Her lips were silent, her voice was weak, but her pussy called out his name loud enough for him to answer.

"Did you miss me, baby?" Jeff asked knowingly, a slight grin covering his face. It was plain to see that she had waited up for him and nothing pleased him more than to come in and find her standing there in her birthday suit. She was absolutely gorgeous. Her brown skin was dusted in a shimmering bronzer that made her look as if she'd been bathing in a tub of corn syrup and toasted in the morning sunlight. Her toned thighs and legs were only a few minutes away from what he knew to be the sexiest and smoothest legs he'd ever felt wrapped around his backside. For a second longer he admired her hair. It was different from the last time he'd seen her. Tonight she presented a more exotic look. Long and straight, jet black silky strands of hair blanketing both her shoulders, her dark nipples playing peek-a-boo through the slits.

Nadine stared her lover up and down. She wondered if he'd just had sex with *her*. The other woman. His wife. She thought about walking over to him, whipping his dick out of his jeans and sniffing it from the head to the nut sac for any aromas distinctive from her own. But decided she could never pull a stunt like that and still convince someone that she was sane.

Jeff walked closer to his mistress, never taking his eyes off her naked physique. He took in as much as he could before wrapping his arms around her tightly. Her skin felt like cotton, it was so soft. He planted kisses on her lips, neck, and shoulders. He was ready to feel her again. They kissed intensely; droplets of rain from his clothes dampened her skin, getting her wet before he could have the chance to. Jeff slid off his leather jacket, then his hat, and laid them across the seat of the recliner.

"I waited up for you," Nadine said.

"I see. But you knew I'd come."

Nadine dropped her head. She did know that, at least she hoped it. "Where is she?" she asked.

"Out with old friends," Jeff said quickly, knowing otherwise. Denise couldn't lie to save her life, but for some reason that didn't bother him much anymore. He told her that he would stay home. Get rested. The only physical contact they had in months was tonight. He gave her a silver pendant to match the diamond earrings he had bought her last year for Mother's Day. She thanked him, tossing it in her panty drawer like some spare change that didn't do her pocketbook any favors. She left a kiss on his cheek as she rushed out the door, dressed to kill in a hip- and ass-hugging black and red dress. One he'd never seen before. Her thigh-high heeled boots covered the majority of skin on her smooth, thick, brown legs. Jeff had to admit she was sexy as hell, but the show wasn't for him. It was for the new man in her life. She had hand-fed him the story all week about going out for Valentine's with a few of her old girlfriends from school. But while Jeff didn't know for a fact if his wife was lying, he gladly used the time to go see his own mistress.

Nadine wasn't as careful with her next question. "So, what time is your curfew tonight?"

Jeff lifted her chin and kissed her tasty lips. "Why don't you let me worry about all that?"

Nadine hated that answer. It made her feel limited and unsure of herself, as though she had no right to be concerned. Her tired and worried gaze settled on his lips. She leaned in for another kiss, along with a nose rub. His touch weakened her, as always. She needed this tonight. Five minutes, ten minutes, she'd take whatever she could get right now. "Make love to me," she whispered with her eyes closed while his gentle and warm kisses moved from her lips, to her chin, neck, and breasts. When it felt this good, it was worth the wait.

Jeff lifted Nadine in his arms and carried her back into the bedroom. He laid her across the unmade queen-sized bed and watched her body sink into the plush pillow-top mattress. She parted her legs and massaged her clit with her own fingers.

Now this is what home felt like, Jeff thought. He was missed. He was wanted. Hell, he was even needed. He undressed quickly, never taking his eyes off his woman. At last, he climbed on top of her warm, naked body.

The entire forty-three minutes Jeff bathed himself inside of

her, all he could think about was having Nadine in his life forever. After a few more strokes, Nadine's screaming orgasm started
with Jeff's only a short distance behind. He pushed himself to her
limits with so much force the iron headboard knocked up against
the wall. He watched Nadine take him and bear the greatness of
the pain as he drove further into her love tunnel. Jeff was so deep
inside Nadine he could feel himself shaking hands with her pelvic
bones. "Awww," he grunted, nearing his peak.

Nadine watched Jeff's eyes roll around in his head. She wrapped
her legs around his back, gripped the rails above her head and
concentrated on surrendering herself to him.

Jeff rocked faster, beads of sweat rolled off his body and on to
her as he pumped out all the energy he had saved for their night.
His eyes met hers and her facial expression spoke volumes. She
was far from being done. "That's it. Right there," she sang, making
his name the ad lib to her song.

Jeff took a glance down at his member. Nadine's juices were so
warm and sticky she drizzled his shaft like frosting on a cake. He
pulled out before he could completely let go, respecting her wishes
of not wanting a slip-up because she wasn't on birth control. He
grabbed for his dick and pumped it until all that overtime came
pouring out in one creamy stream and onto Nadine's smooth flat
belly. She laid spent and satisfied. "Happy Valentine's Day," he
said before kissing her lips again.

Nadine just smiled back at him. "Ditto," she replied softly,
looking back over at the clock.

"I have to go," Jeff said. "But I'll call you tomorrow." He gave her
another reassuring kiss, rose from the bed, and started to dress.

5

*D*enise allowed Greg to examine her caramel-brown, voluptuous body from head to toe, just the way he had so many times before. The only entertainment Denise seemed to be getting tonight was from her own thoughts. *Oh how I just love this man! I'm not sure what he's waiting on but any day now he's going to ask me to leave Jeff for him and become his wife.*

Greg was sitting at the edge of the bed taking in all of her body. He hadn't laid a single finger on her yet and her pussy was playing the drums. It was no secret that just his being here was enough to turn her on. To validate that thought a puddle of love juice formed underneath her, transforming the spot where she lay into a warm soak in a Jacuzzi.

"I'm so wet," Denise moaned, hoping that would be enough to get Greg out of his clothes and in the bed with her. "I only get this wet when you're around."

Greg said nothing, just eyed her large breasts in the satiny sapphire strapless bra that she deliberately bought a whole cup size too small. It covered just the lower half of both her breasts, but Denise didn't mind the temporary discomfort. She wanted her breasts to look the way they had in college—round and firm. Void of stretch marks. The new enhancement she wore tonight exceeded all of her past efforts by a long shot. Her breasts sat so perfectly on top of her chest that Greg wouldn't recognize the difference if his life depended on it. But even with all the breasts and ass laying there at his mercy, why hadn't he made one move on her yet?

"You look so beautiful, baby," Greg finally complimented after being in Denise's presence for all of twenty-three minutes. He leaned in and planted a sensual kiss on her glossed lips.

Denise maneuvered her tongue into Greg's mouth. Her kisses were passionate and represented how she felt below the waist.

Greg interrupted the passion, imagining Denise's plump lips pleasing him in a more appreciated place. He could feel himself rising to the occasion. Still, he pulled back.

Denise held her breath, ready to burst with desire. The seductive look in her eyes should have given Greg a clue of what she wanted, but it was obvious his attention was elsewhere. She decided she'd eliminate the guesswork for him. He must be exhausted from work, she told herself, cooking up ways to help him relax. "Why don't you get comfortable," she said, smiling, batting her long false eyelashes. She reached for a pineapple chunk from the assorted arrangement of fruit she'd brought into the bedroom. Her mouth watered from the taste of strawberries and champagne. She needed Greg to get with the program. She'd been waiting all week for this night to happen, paying her mother to keep her daughter for the night, concocting a phony alibi about old friends from college to satisfy any curiosity Jeff might have. So considering all of her efforts, Denise wanted to make every minute of her time with Greg count. In addition to that, Greg had wined and dined her with lavish gifts all week and it was time for her to thank him, in her own special way.

Their eyes shifted away from each other before finding their way back. "Umm," Denise moaned, dragging her tongue over her upper lip. "Tasty." She took another bite. "Join me." She kept her focus on the hunk of chocolate before her. Greg had smooth dark skin, dark dreamy brown eyes, and a million-dollar smile to match his million-dollar pockets. If Denise wasn't personally managing his investment portfolio, didn't know his real name, she would have thought he was related to Blair Underwood. Greg resembled the actor and had an amazing body for a forty-one-year-old. She couldn't ask for more.

Yet, Greg remained disconnected, unsure of how to respond to Denise. Had he known it would be this damn hard to leave, he would have just cancelled their plans over the phone. He would have told her he had an emergency, a valid excuse that he knew she'd accept with no questions asked. Had he thought to do that, he chided himself; he wouldn't be in this predicament. He carefully traced around Denise's navel with his fingertips, trying his best to ignore her last request. He watched how her body responded to his every touch, swallowed his guilt, and tried to focus on how he would say what he'd been keeping from her for the three years they'd been sleeping together.

"What's wrong, baby?" Denise asked as she sucked the pineapple juice off her thumb. The way her eyebrows converged, she looked as though she had a thick and defined unibrow. Denise couldn't take the silent treatment any longer. It wasn't like Greg. She took her right hand and placed it over his. When he didn't respond, her worry ratcheted up. Was he turned off by her new perfume? "Talk to me, baby." Nothing. Maybe it was her hair. That had to be it. The big bouncy curls surely reminded him of some old woman, she imagined, feeling insecure all of a sudden. She rose from her laid-back position, then patted down her curls. "I hope it's not me."

Greg turned away from her. He couldn't tell her. She wasn't ready and neither was he.

"Greg?"

Denise wouldn't let this rest. He had to say something. He began dropping off the first lie that came to his mind. "Of course it's not you. I just remembered that I have an appointment with one of my clients. She's only here in town for the week. I'm really not prepared for her."

Denise looked down at her watch. "This late?" The sparkling glow she once held in her eyes, vanished.

Greg nodded his head; an underlying mask of shame shattered the truth in one firm and solid, "Yes."

There was a thought-smothering moment of silence. The temperature in the room dropped from a simmering hot to an icy cold, and the river of heat that flowed from between Denise's legs dried up like the Atacama Desert. She tried her best to disguise her disappointment. "I see. Well, I guess we'll just have to pick this up another time…" A faint smile swept her wet lips as she went in to kiss him. "…when your schedule allows."

Greg allowed the uneasiness that crept through his body to render him wordless. Or maybe it was the text message he received a half an hour ago. The one that had him cursing out the woman who'd sent it, over and over in his mind. He shifted his body away from Denise's so she couldn't question him about the new vibration coming from his jacket. Another text message.

Denise watched Greg closely, disappointment returning to her all at once. "Aren't you going to answer that? It could be your client."

Greg rose to his feet. He didn't want to leave but he had to. He was at war with his conscience, for sure. It told him that he needed to tell her, at least give her the choice to stay or leave. The vibration surfed through his pocket again. "I better go," he managed.

"Here. Don't forget this," she said, handing him his gift. The rectangular box was wrapped neatly in silver gift foil. No bow, instead the red lipstick imprint of her lush lips.

"I told you not to buy me anything."

Denise gave him a devilish grin. "What are you going to do about it? Spank me?"

Greg smiled, leaned in, and planted a kiss on her cheek. "I'll call you," he promised. He turned around and headed for the front door. His cell was still going crazy and still he ignored the person calling him. He rushed for the elevator door, catching it on its way down.

The second the doors opened, Greg stormed out of the elevator, shoulder-bumping a few hotel guests in passing. "Pardon me," he called out. He raced down the short flight of steps and through the dark parking garage. He stopped in his tracks, trying to remember exactly where he had parked. Following the signage, he picked up his pace until he came to the fifth row. He reached in his jacket then and pulled out his phone. The alerts for several missed calls and texts registered on the screen. Greg jumped in his sleek Rolls-Royce Phantom and sped out of the garage. He punched in a number. Predictably so, a woman answered on the first ring. Greg took a deep breath. "I'm on my way." Before he could say anything more, he was getting an earful from the other end. Bad reception made the woman sound even more annoying than just her voice alone. "I said, I'm on my way, Vivian!" His tone rose with every syllable. "One of my appointments ran over."

"Aghhh! Don't give me that. As a matter of fact, don't even bother, Greg," Vivian hissed at him. She went on and on about how she had already left the airport. How he'd neglected to pick her up, even though he knew she'd be coming in on an earlier flight. She complained about the filthiness of the cab she had to take and how Greg's disregard to her welfare was so irresponsible. She told him he needed to rearrange his priorities. Reminding him that she was his wife. She always came first.

Vivian stopped her nagging and bitching, only to take her frustrations out on her driver instead. "Excuse me, mister. Do you care to slow it down in all this rain?" she spat with attitude. "Are you trying to kill me?" she said accusingly.

The driver looked down at the speedometer and then in the rearview mirror at her and rolled his eyes. He was only driving forty-five and the speed limit was sixty. "I wouldn't put you in harm's way, ma'am."

Vivian huffed under her breath. Was he talking back to her? She made a mental note to report him first thing in the morning.

Greg let out a frustrating sigh. He didn't feel like dealing with Vivian's shit tonight. "Are you going to be in this sour-ass mood all night?" he asked before he knew it.

"Fuck you! I just buried my mother," she cried. "And all you can think to ask me is if I'm going to be in a sour-ass mood all night?" She waited. Greg offered no response or apology. "Out of the six months I spent in Connecticut, you didn't think to come visit me once. You knew mother was getting sicker. I told you and you couldn't even be there for me!"

"You know damn well your parents never cared to have me around, so quit pretending, Vivian! Your mother has hated me since the day she met me, let alone the eleven years we've been married. So tell me what difference these past six months were going to make?" He waited for Vivian to enlighten him. "I didn't think you could."

"That's not true and you know it! Mother accepted you into our family. They both did! Who do you think invested the seed money to start Adams Companies, huh?" Vivian lashed out in defense.

The cab driver stared back at his ivory-skinned, distraught passenger. Women like her always had issues. His annoyed expression was as visible as the sheets of rain that fell from the dark sky.

"You were always so accusatory toward my parents when they wanted nothing but the best for you," Vivian spat. She met eyes with the driver, asking herself how in the hell was he paying attention to the road when his eyes were on her. She became more infuriated.

"Yeah, okay. Keep telling yourself whatever you need to if it helps you sleep better at night, Vivian. They wanted the best for *you*. That's why they gave *us* the money! And had I known that money came from them, I would have never accepted it!" Greg admitted. All this time he thought Vivian had gotten a loan from the bank. At least that's what she had told him.

"Yeah, right! And if I didn't know any better, I would have thought it was all in your plans when you married me," she spat spitefully.

Greg balled his fist tightly and inhaled deeply to prevent him from saying something he'd later regret.

"Second house on the left," Vivian directed the driver. "I'm home now, Greg. Where are you?" That quickly the argument was dismissed. They could go on and on about this the way they always seemed to do, but she didn't feel like the emotional train ride tonight. She had just lost the most loving person in the world to her and her husband acted as though he didn't give a shit. Vivian didn't understand Greg's attitude. Why couldn't he just leave the past behind and be there for her in her time of need?

Greg watched discreetly from a short distance as the cab driver quickly unloaded Vivian's luggage onto their front porch. He witnessed her sandy blonde hair fall victim to the rain. She hadn't used an umbrella. His entire body stiffened. The six months she'd been away did him some good. It gave him the opportunity to put things into perspective. Before her mother's illness began to take a toll on their marriage three years ago, he was a faithful, loving husband, but things had changed all at once. Vivian changed. He changed. And now, he didn't really know where he fit into her life. Or where she fit into his.

Vivian carefully counted the large designer suitcases on her porch to ensure they were all accounted for. She thought about tipping the poor illegal immigrant driver, but decided against it. He was rude to her and didn't deserve a dime of her money. "Thank you!" she hollered out to him. The look plastered on his face told her she could have kept her empty words because she wasn't at all welcomed. She watched him angrily reverse out of her circular cobblestone driveway and back onto the streets, away from their quiet posh multimillion-dollar estate. A plethora of rain followed. She fumbled in her purse for her keys. The distressed look on her face unveiled the heart-aching pain she'd tried to cope with since the funeral. Finally, after three key tries, Vivian was able to unlock the door. Remembering her husband was still on the other end of the line, she said, "Where'd you say you were again?"

"Not far," Greg said, trying to determine whether or not he should give her a few minutes to herself.

"Well, I'm going to freshen up, take some aspirin, and pray that my headache goes away," Vivian said. "I'll see you when you get here. Just try not to make too much noise if I'm already asleep."

Greg withdrew the words resting at the foot of his mouth and instead buttered up the words, "Okay, baby. Get some rest because you've had a long flight. I promise not to disturb your sleep. In fact, I'll be so quiet that you won't even know I'm there."

Vivian agreeably pressed END and walked completely inside her cozy home.

6

*D*enise had dozed off. If it wasn't for her cell phone blaring one of her favorite Jill Scott songs, she never would have budged. She pulled the brown leather case from out of her purse. "Hello," she answered, hoping it wasn't her husband calling to question her about what time she would be coming home. She'd pressed the button so quickly she hadn't gotten a chance to see whose number was on the screen.

"Sweetheart?"

"Hey you," Denise said, clearing her throat. She pulled herself up. "Is everything okay? Did your appointment show?" She looked around the suite. From the panoramic view the open curtains provided, she could see the rain falling harder than before.

"Yeah, they made it. I'm going in now," Greg said.

Denise had been hoping they would have cancelled. She wanted Greg with her tonight. "Okay. Well, good luck and I hope everything turns out well for you."

At first Greg didn't respond. Not until he reached the floor of their presidential suite. "I hate that I couldn't stay."

"Don't worry about it," she said, sighing. "Business comes before pleasure."

"Is that so?" he asked her.

Denise jumped suddenly because the voice on the phone was back in her suite. She hadn't moved an inch since he left. She dropped her legs over the side of the bed and rose to her feet. She couldn't control the excitement throbbing between her sticky thighs. "So does this mean I'm the client tonight?" she asked him in her sultry voice, hoping that the answer would be yes.

Greg placed both of his hands on the sides of her face and gazed into her eyes. Her caramel skin was as velvety as whipped butter. His lips fell over hers. She tasted like a combination of pineapple, mango, strawberry and melon, with a hint of champagne. Denise had started the party without him but he was definitely going to finish it. He rubbed his hands over her ass, up the small of her back, and then cradled her neck. His tongue maneuvered its way through her fruity-flavored lips. He snatched off his tie, slid off his jacket and unbuttoned his shirt. Denise assisted him along the way by undoing his belt and unsnapping his pants. Once his pants hit the floor, down came his boxers. Not once did they interrupt their tongues.

Denise felt herself melting in his hands and yet she couldn't describe that wonderful feeling any more than the four letter word that seemed to say it all. She backed her way onto the inviting king-sized bed. The red and pink candy-scented rose petals still decorated the designer sheets. Denise wiggled her way to the middle, laid on her back, and enjoyed every second of the moment as Greg slowly slid down her panties. With one hand he eased them from around both of her ankles. "Awwww," she moaned, feeling her pussy awaken. Greg planted kisses all over her squirming body as he undressed. He knew how to make her feel good. She opened her thick brown thighs as wide as they would spread. She was just as wet as before. She grabbed both of his arms as he pushed himself inside her. "It feels so good," she said in between breaths.

Greg moved his mouth to Denise's right nipple. It seemingly

jumped out of her bra at him. He licked and sucked on it while caressing the other that stayed put. He wasn't even inside of her that long and he felt himself about to explode. Along with that warning, his thrusts picked up pace until Denise's nails were piercing his backside. She was in her highest falsetto but he refused to weaken his stroke.

Oh he fucks me sooo good! Denise yodeled over and over in her mind.

Greg gave her the head-start she needed but now his nut was chasing hers down. He gave it to her slow, fast, and rough—just how she liked it. He lifted her legs high in the air. "Damn, you feel so good."

Sweat rolled down the sides of Greg's face. Denise was used to it by now. He was a water boy, just like her husband. She snatched off the pillowcase from one of the bedside pillows and blotted his forehead with it. She wildly bucked her hips from underneath him, competing with his every movement. She felt like a cowgirl at a rodeo show. In fact, she got so into her character that both her breasts practically leaped out of her bra and started bouncing all over the place.

Greg watched her make the face she always made when she was reaching her climax. He began moving with a new motion until he was hitting her G-spot.

"Greg!" she moaned, louder.

Denise closed her eyes, feeling dizzy from the rush. Her walls had caved in on him, holding Greg as her personal prisoner. She pussy-gripped his dick tighter than a glove, squeezing every bit of the love offering out of him, until he was coming. He got up, slid off the condom he'd been wearing, and dropped it in the nearby wastebasket. When he walked back over to Denise, she had the chilled champagne bottle in her hand. She took in a mouthful, got on her knees, and bent over until his midsection was dead in her face. She placed both her hands on the edge of the bed for balance as she knelt before him and took his manhood into her mouth. The coolness from the bubbly instantly woke him as she marinated his shaft in Dom Pérignon. The slurping and the gurgling drove him crazy and he began pumping her mouth.

For a full hour, with no hands, Denise sucked Greg off like a porno star. She felt so kinky when she was with him. Her next act would steal the show. Watching his head fall back as her talented tongue showered his dick, she immediately took her right hand and massaged his balls until another full shot of warm creamy lava began filling her mouth.

7

"*Y*ou are wearing that pantsuit, Mrs. Jackson! Plum is definitely your color." Tonya complimented Denise the second her boss entered through the double glass doors into the outer office area. She watched Denise strut her stuff, greeting everyone in the hallway with a huge smile and a formal nod of the head before finally making her way to Tonya's desk.

"Thank you, Tonya," Denise said, smiling back at her secretary who also looked professionally stunning in a jade dress accessorized with a wide black belt that accentuated her waistline. Her short and wavy, honey blonde hair was combed back simply. One karat diamond solitaire earrings lit up the newlywed's smooth high-yellow complexion.

Denise positioned her hands on the corners of the glass desk. "Any messages for me?"

Tonya minimized the spreadsheet on her screen and double-clicked the Outlook icon. She glanced over her notes. "Yes. Christina called with the updates on the Humphrey's accounts, and…" She tabbed over. "Mr. Craddock has the financials you requested."

"Wonderful. Could you call him back and make sure those get forwarded to my email as soon as possible?"

"You got it."

Denise started for her office, four-inch heels echoing across the marble floors as she moved. Platinum Crest Investments was thriving where many of their competitors had failed. The economic crisis had made business challenging. Still, Denise and Nadine managed to acquire two new large accounts since all the recession talk, and were working on number three. So for Denise and Nadine, life couldn't be sweeter. As an afterthought she reminded herself to check on Nadine. She peeked inside her best friend's dimly lit office. The large glass desk Nadine often sat behind was neatly organized and not a fingerprint smudge could be found on it. While Nadine would never admit it, she had suffered from an obsessive cleaning disorder. Everything had to be spotless.

Denise walked over to Nadine's credenza, pulled a neon green sticky note from a notepad dispenser and wrote, "Let's Do Lunch." Artistically challenged, she endorsed it with a smiley face and attached the note to the middle of Nadine's computer monitor. They were both swamped with work and had busy personal lives, too. As a result, they hadn't seen much of each other lately. It was time they did some catching up.

Denise started for her office, grabbing a cup of freshly brewed Starbucks coffee from the break room along the way. It was early so most of the staff hadn't made it in yet. Unless there was a meeting, Denise never saw their faces before nine. Stepping inside of her spacious office suite, she immediately felt warm. She placed her Louis Vuitton briefcase on her desk and walked over to the thermostat to adjust the temperature. She pulled back the blinds covering her panoramic windows and a gorgeous view of downtown Dallas emerged. It was amazing how much of the city you could see from thirty-two floors above ground level. Her corner office anchored the downtown Dallas arts district and overlooked the skyline amongst the plentiful array of fancy architectural office buildings, brownstones, luxurious hotels, nightclubs and eateries.

Her forty-seven-floor tower housed many of the high-end law firms, real estate agencies, developers, a bank, and headquarters for many corporations. She was constantly surrounded by wealth and growing businesses.

It didn't take long for Denise to cool off and get into the daily groove of things. She found her brain working overtime, but somehow Greg managed to intercept her thoughts. She wondered what he was doing. Wondered if he missed her as much as she missed him. Granted they'd seen each other almost every day since Valentine's, still Denise couldn't get enough of him. She was addicted to the quality time they shared, the attention he gave her, and best of all, the love they made. She felt a strong chemistry with Greg. Not only was he charismatic, intelligent, business-minded, and one of the wealthiest black men in America, but he also shared her viewpoints. They could sit and hold an intellectual conversation about the day's economy, the stock market, and the financial crisis, whereas with Jeff, it was as if she was speaking a foreign language whenever she broached those subjects.

Greg's conversation stimulated her in more places than one and was far more satisfying than even having intercourse with her husband. Greg taught her things and she admired him for that. He also took the time to learn everything about her. He knew her favorite drink, her favorite television show, even knew her smallest of habits. All this and he didn't even live in the same household. It made her question her relationship with her husband all the more. There was so much missing between them. However, when she laid down with Greg, the missing pieces found their way to her. She was compatible with Greg. And the fact that he was a successful multi-millionaire didn't hurt. He was the CEO and Chairman of Adams Companies, the largest African-American hotel group in America, fourteen hotels in twelve different cities. He had even been profiled on CNN's *Black In America* special. She was dating a man with status and ambition. Money and power.

Denise snatched up the receiver, a tingling sensation gnawing at her insides just from the mere thought of her lover. She straightened her posture, brought the phone closer to her ear and dialed Greg's number. The anticipation traveled from her fingers to her pussy as she pressed each number firmly. It rang several times before his voicemail picked up. She decided against leaving a message, knowing the desperation would be discerned in her voice. She tried to take her mind off of Greg for just a moment, and instead stared at the large group of numbers on her computer screen. She was supposed to be reviewing a prospect's financials, hoping to find a fit for her services when the phone rang, further sidetracking her concentration. It was Tonya.

"Mrs. Jackson, I'm sorry to bother you, but I have your mom on the other line," Tonya said. "Should I ask her to call you back?"

It was barely nine o'clock. Denise wondered what her mother could have possibly wanted this early. "No, put her through, please." Once the second light disappeared, indicating that Tonya had cleared her end, Denise began to speak. "Morning, Ma," she said, half-enthused.

"Don't you 'Morning Ma' me!" Grace said. "Where is my money, Miss Thang?"

Denise chuckled at the mention of her mother calling her Miss Thang. She swore her mother had a new nickname every time they talked. "Ma, I will bring it today, as soon as I leave work." Denise took a few seconds to mentally calculate what she owed. Her mom had only charged her because she made her miss Bingo night. "Wait a minute. You mean to tell me you're calling me about a measly twenty-five dollars?"

Her mother was tickled at the thought as well. "Well, it's *my* measly twenty-five dollars and I'll sweat you for it as much as I like." She laughed again. "Speaking of *my* money, how's my grand-baby?" Grace hadn't seen her in three days.

"She's fine."

"That's good. Well, I hate to rush but I told Betty I'd take her to the grocery store. So I better get a move on before she come beating down my door with that cane."

"Okay, see you later, Ma." Denise laughed before her mother could hang up. She shook her head. Her mother was a trip but she loved her to death and would do anything for her. She hoped for the same relationship with her own daughter.

"What are you so happy about this morning?" Nadine asked. She leaned against the doorframe, her smile just as broad as Denise's, glancing over at the beautiful outside view Denise had from her office window. She remembered how they'd played a childish game of rock-paper-scissors to determine who would get that office.

Denise stood from her chair, rounded her desk. "I haven't seen you in ages!" she said, hugging her friend. "You would think we didn't work right next door to each other."

"I know. I've just had so much going on lately," Nadine stated, knowing she'd been intentionally avoiding Denise. She stood frozen in a cemented block of shame that prevented her from looking Denise in the eye. "I love this color on you. And are you losing weight?"

Denise tugged at the corners of her jacket, then slowly rocked in a full spin. "I believe I am," she said, grateful that somebody noticed. That meant her early morning walks were paying off. "I think I'm losing it pretty quickly, too." She paused. "Well, enough about me, what's been up with you?" She led Nadine by the hand and nearly forced her in a chair while she took the seat beside her.

Nadine peered out the window once again, pretending to be too caught up in the view to have heard Denise. "I've always loved this office."

"Hey, I beat you fair and square." Denise laughed, pointing her index finger at Nadine. They both looked at the phone when it rang. Denise reached over to catch the call.

"Mrs. Jackson, there's a Gregory Adams holding on line one," Tonya said.

"I need to take this," Denise mouthed to Nadine.

Nadine lifted herself to her feet. She smiled back at her friend, whispering that they could catch up later. She excused herself out of the office, shutting the door behind her.

"Put him through, please," Denise said finally. She greeted Greg in her sexiest tone. "Hello. I was just sitting here missing you."

"I can't imagine more than I've missed you?" Greg said.

"Oh, well, you better imagine it because it's the truth."

Greg was smiling inside. He loved to hear her talk like that. He thought he heard his wife coming up the stairs and remembered the real reason he decided to return Denise's missed call. "We need to talk."

Denise felt a smile creeping over her face. "About?"

Greg felt his wife's presence getting closer. "Us," he said briefly.

A warm fuzzy feeling shot through Denise's body. "Okay. When?"

"Greg!" a female's voice called out. Greg turned on the faucet in the bathroom to drown out his conversation. "Tonight."

Immediately, Denise knew her wish would come true after all. She looked forward to the next time they would be together and the timing was perfect. She had an outfit already in mind. "Tonight's good for me," she said quickly.

The voice called out to him again. "Greg!"

Denise heard the female's voice sailing through the phone line. "Sounds like someone's trying to get your attention."

Greg's words clung to his lips. "My client's here," he said in a faint whisper. "I'll call you around seven."

Denise barely got out an, "Okay," before Greg disconnected the call. She was too excited to ask questions, think twice, or allow her woman's intuition to interfere with the feeling that swept over her. Greg was a good man, a better man than any she'd ever known, and she refused to think differently. She closed her eyes for only a second, then opened them when her door eased back open.

"I'm going to wrap up and go home," Nadine said weakly.

"Are you okay?" Denise asked, concerned.

"My stomach's been bothering me. Think I might be coming down with the swine flu." She wiped her sweaty palm across her forehead. She was warm.

"Swine flu? Girl, please tell me you're joking," Denise said, pulling out a can of Lysol from under her desk. She definitely could not afford to get sick.

"I'm not quite sure what it is but, lately, I haven't been feeling well," Nadine replied in a near whisper.

Denise noticed the seriousness in her friend's tone, the lack of vitality in her posture, the flush in her skin. "You *don't* look well either, now that you mention it," Denise agreed. "You should go. Check with your doctor if you need to. And call me if you need anything."

"Thank you," Nadine told her. "I'm going to go straight home and take some medicine. Hopefully I'll feel better by tomorrow. If not, I'll go see the doctor and see what's going on."

Just as Nadine was about to close the door behind her, Denise called out, "Nay!"

Nadine peeked her head back inside. "What's up?"

"You know you're my only best friend, right?"

Nadine gave Denise a puzzled look. "Of course," she said.

"If I told you something, would you look at me any differently?"

Now Nadine was really confused. "Why would I do that?" Denise had entrusted her with things before. A much deeper secret that she still kept to this day.

Denise knew this wasn't the place to discuss her personal affairs, but she felt it was time to tell Nadine about Greg. Her phone rang again. It was Tonya transferring another call. This was a call she definitely had to take. She looked at Nadine's expression and motioned for her to go ahead and leave.

"Are you sure?" Nadine mouthed. "I can wait until you're off the phone."

Denise nodded her head, turning her attention away from Nadine and to the caller on the other end of the line. "Mr. Humphrey. Just the man I've been looking for."

Nadine smiled at Denise and closed her door. Maybe they could talk about it later, but right now, she had to get out of there. Suddenly everything around her made her sick.

8

"So…Canvas Green," Jeff started, glancing down at the name on the application. "Give me one good reason why I should hire you." The young man sitting directly across from Jeff was wearing a dingy white wife-beater, black jeans that hung off his ass, and red tennis shoes with missing shoe laces. Jeff couldn't believe he was actually giving the young cat the time of day, considering how he waltzed up in here looking for a job dressed so inappropriately. Didn't he realize that was an insult to Jeff and his business?

"Well, you should hire me 'cause I'm good at selling shit, I mean stuff," he quickly corrected.

Jeff allowed the response to soak in. It was almost as though he could see the life this young man was headed for, and for some odd reason, he felt he could detour that path. "Stand up, young man," Jeff said.

The guy stood to his feet. The cornrows that fell to his shoulders were the neatest thing on his body. With his back straight and feet positioned side by side, he wasn't sure what Jeff was going to ask him to do. He stared Jeff straight in the eye. The two were almost equals. Same height, give or take an inch, same build, both handsome. They could have passed for brothers on the street. Hell, he could have even been his father, the boy thought, considering how he didn't know him.

Jeff remained in his seat, unimpressed. "I tell you what. Walk right on out that door you came in, go home, then ask your parents how you should dress for a job interview. After you do all of that, then you can come back and have a grown man conversation with me."

The young man stared at Jeff as though he was crazy. "Man, I ain't got no parents to ask anything. It's just me and my baby sister," the boy said. "I'm the parents." His eyes were glossed over. "I just need a stable income to get on my feet."

Jeff's jaws nearly hit the floor. How in hell was this wet-behind-the-ears Salvation Army mascot going to walk up in his place of business expecting a handout? Jeff wished he could knock some nigga-sense into his little ass. "So you think I'm supposed to feel sorry for you?" Jeff chuckled, his game face competing with his contender's.

Standing on his proud feet, the young man took a step backwards. "Say man, I ain't looking for no charity. I'm just trying to earn a decent living so my sister and I don't end up homeless. That's it, aiight. Whatever work you got, I'll take," he said. "I'll even sweep and mop the sidewalks if that's all the work you have. I just need something to hold us over until this music thing come through for me." Canvas beamed. "You should check out my demo. I got mad skills," he added confidently.

Jeff was amused. *The audacity of some people*, he thought. He crossed his arms over one another and leaned back in his chair, trying to figure out the young boy, but unable to. His guard was up and he wouldn't let Jeff see past the outer appearance, an appearance that Jeff had already stereotyped him for; a project thug looking for a quick come up. Jeff would bet his BMW that the boy sold weed, dope, and just about everything under the sun to support himself and his sister. He couldn't help wondering how old the little girl was and how they landed in such a predicament. "Sit back down," he said, motioning for the chair.

The young man pulled up his sagging Coogi jeans and took a seat.

"How old are you?" Jeff asked.

The boy hesitated before he rattled off his age. "Seventeen."

"Seventeen!" Jeff gave him a second once-over. *What in the hell are these young cats drinking nowadays*, he thought. "If you want to earn your way on my payroll, you have to prove yourself. Starting with"—he looked the young man up and down—"those clothes."

Canvas looked down at his attire. This was his street gear. But he wouldn't allow changing up the look to be a problem at all. "Don't worry. This won't be an issue," he assured Jeff.

"Well, we'll see about that. Tomorrow. Eleven a.m. sharp."

"I got the job?" the boy asked, ecstatic at the thought.

Jeff stood from his chair. "No. But what you do have is another opportunity to prove to me that you can represent this company."

The boy came to his feet and extended a warm handshake. "Thanks, brotha!"

Without smiling, Jeff tightened his grip. "Just call me Mr. Jackson."

Jeff pulled up at Grace's house, four on the dot. His mother-in-law, a gray-haired spitting image of Denise, rocked back and forth in an old rocking chair on her porch as she knitted away on the quilt strewn over her lap. She didn't hear or notice Jeff getting out of his car and making his way up the cracked pavement until Deandra came running out of the house, arms flailing, screaming, "Daddy!" at the top of her young lungs. She had already changed out of her school uniform and was now in her play gear. A pink and white shirt with blue jean shorts.

"There's Daddy's big girl!" Jeff said, scooping his nine-year-old in his arms and squeezing her tight.

"Where's Mama?" Deandra asked her father. Her two twisted pigtails rocked with her head movement.

Jeff could not care less but he offered his daughter the explanation Denise had given him. "She had to work late," he said. "Now go on and grab your things because I have a surprise for you."

"You do?" Deandra asked, jumping up and down with excitement. She loved surprises, especially those that came from her daddy. She shot back in the house.

"Quit runnin' before you fall and hurt yourself, chile!" Grace shouted, smiling as she shook her head.

Jeff took a seat beside Grace in the wicker chair.

"So Denise tells me you're doing pretty good for yourself over there at the, um, um..."

"Lexus dealership," Jeff completed.

"Yeah, that's it. She says you sell a lot of cars. Think you can do anything with that one over there?" Grace pointed to her brown 1980 station wagon. "It's a classic," she added, gazing at the clunker in her driveway over the bifocals that rested on the bridge of her nose. She hadn't seen one like it in years and it still lasted longer than all the men she'd ever laid up with put together.

"I'll see what I can do."

"I'm ready, Daddy!" Deandra said, anxious to know what the surprise was.

"Well, Grace, we're gonna skip on out of here. I hate to leave good company," he said, smiling, rising from the chair. "But me and my baby girl here are going on a little date."

"My, my. How special that's going to be," Grace said, eyeing the pair. "Well, where's my suga, little girl?"

Deandra wrapped her arms around her grandmother's neck and let her kiss her pudgy little cheeks.

"All right. Y'all have fun now," Grace said, waving the two of them off.

Jeff pulled away from the curb and headed toward the Main Event, a huge entertainment center filled with video arcades, bowling, food, and much more. He knew they'd have all the fun in the world. It also gave him the chance to wine and dine his favorite girl for a change.

adine slowly pulled herself up from the living room sofa. Judging from the darkness in the room, she knew it was late. She had overslept after allowing herself what was supposed to be a quick power-nap to recover some of the energy she'd lost. Between all the vomiting and fatigue, she never truly understood what the phrase "under the weather" meant, until now. She couldn't recall ever being this sick except for the minor colds or asthma attacks she had as a child. Otherwise, she was health- and body-conscious. Her philosophical outlook on why people got sick was simply because they neglected to take care of themselves. She, however, didn't fit into that category. That explained why she was starting to worry.

She tossed the chenille fur throw to the side and stood to her aching bare feet. They were beyond sensitive. It felt as though she was walking on pinecones as she slowly made her way toward the gourmet kitchen. Her entire condominium, decorated in Chinese-inspired modern art, replicated her eclectic taste. Porcelain china decorated her black, marble countertops, while squared glass plates and bowls embellished her cherrywood cabinetry. She walked over to the fridge and pulled out a bottle of Evian spring water. In seemingly one gulp, it was all gone.

Nadine stayed still long enough to hear the vibrating noise that called out to her from her purse. She rushed back over to the spot she camped out on the very moment she hit the door, only to have missed the call by a push of a button. It was Jeff. She wanted to call him back, ask him to come over, but something stopped her before her thumb could scroll over the first digit. How much longer was she going to allow this to go on? Because it seemed that during all of this, she was the only one affected. On second thought, her battered feelings didn't deserve the time of day. She knew that it was Denise who would suffer the most if she ever found out about them.

Once again, Nadine was devastated. She couldn't even be in the same room with her friend or hold a normal conversation without feeling like some lying thief. She almost hated herself for it. Why? Why was she betraying her only true friend? Nadine wished she could blame someone else. Jeff came to mind first. It was him, she thought. She should have never let him seduce her that night in the parking lot. She should have told Denise. Got it all out then and dealt with the consequences head on.

Nadine took a deep breath. She was going to drive herself crazy at the rate she was going. She'd always known a time would come when everything that they'd done in the dark would make its way into the light. That much she did believe. She could feel that timing creeping in on her, backing her against a wall with her hands tied. It was frightening knowing that she'd have to force her feelings aside and focus on getting the truth out of her system once and for all. After she mustered up the strength, she would look Denise dead in the eyes and say, "I've been sleeping with your husband." Nadine knew the second that prolonged echo of a thought would register with Denise, that their friendship would be history, their partnership would be a has-been, and she and Denise would both continue on with their lives as enemies. That much Nadine expected, and that much she tried to prepare herself for. There wouldn't be anything that she could say that would change the past or the present. Not even the *I'm sorry* she'd squeeze out just before getting the shit slapped out of her.

Another vibration sent her BlackBerry spinning around on the console, pulling her out of deep thought. She had a voicemail alert. Several of them. After punching in her birthdate as her pin code, she sat back down and retrieved all her messages. Most of them from clients with the exception of the last one. It was from Jeff.

"Hey, baby, it's me," Jeff said, his words almost sporadic. "I was talking to Denise and she mentioned that you left early. I hope everything's okay."

Nadine pressed the phone closer to her ear, trying to make out every word over the background noise.

"I've just had a lot on my mind lately. You. Denise. Deandra."

Nadine scooted to the edge of the couch, dropping her head almost in her lap. She counted an eight-second pause before he started up again.

"I can't figure this shit out right now for the life of me. All I know is I love having you in my life and that other than my daughter, you're the best thing that has ever happened to me." He was interrupted. "I need more tokens, Daddy!"

Nadine picked up on the child's voice. It was Deandra.

"Daddy will be right there, sweetheart."

Nadine didn't bother wiping the salty tears that began to collect on her face.

"Nadine, I have to be honest with you. I've never felt this way before. And I don't want to have you this way. In a lie…"

Nadine paced her breaths. She wished he'd go ahead and spit it out. The quieter he got, the louder the young voices grew. All she could hear now were kids laughing, crying, playing, and shouting. It sounded like an indoor playground.

"I want to share my world with you. All of it. Without the boundaries. Without hiding in secret." Pause. "So, it's about time Denise knew about us. I won't keep putting you through this…"

Beep. "Press one to save this message or two to delete."

By the time the operator was giving her instructions, Nadine was already dialing Jeff's number from the house phone. Her calls were going straight to voicemail. "Shit!" she cursed. She couldn't let him do it. Denise needed to hear it from her. She needed her to understand how sorry she was. Needed her to know she never meant to hurt her. That the affair sort of just happened. That she couldn't control how she felt. That she'd fallen in love.

She tried Jeff's number again. Voicemail. She called him a total of nine times, leaving message after message for him to return her calls. Her heart was beating fast. A trillion beats for every millisecond. She began to sweat. She needed her asthma pump but couldn't find it fast enough. She had taken it out of her purse because she'd gone months without having an attack. Now she was having one. She rushed for her bathroom. Snatching open the medicine cabinet, her fingers reached for the blue and white inhaler. She stuck it in her mouth and began squirting out the maximum dosage. She closed her eyes, tilted her head back and allowed the medicine to enter her system. She inhaled and exhaled in deep long breaths until her breathing returned to normal. Nadine started for the phone, dialing Jeff's number once again. She couldn't let him do this. It wasn't time.

This little girl is heavy, Jeff thought as he carried his sleeping daughter into the house. She had played herself out and so had he. Combined, their ticket count added up to well over eight hundred, and that didn't compare to the stash Deandra kept in the treasure box under her bed. Tickets she'd stashed from their last visit to Main Event. She was saving up for one of the gigantic prizes she had told him.

Jeff walked into her room, flipping up the light switch that turned on her Walt Disney bedside lamp. One of her favorite Christmas gifts ever. The whole room was overdone in the *Princess and the Frog* theme. He pulled back the oversized twin comforter with Disney's beautiful black princess, Tiana, posed across the front, and laid Deandra flat on her back. He slid off her shoes and socks and watched her pretty little toes wiggle their way underneath the blanket. Jeff cleared Deandra's bangs out of her face and kissed her softly on the cheek. His baby girl was the reason he decided to man up and marry Denise. She was the reason he dropped out of college on a basketball scholarship, only to land a sales job that paid him commission only. Deandra was also the reason why he stayed in the marriage as long as he did. Nine years of hell was all for his daughter.

Jeff began to mentally sift through the chapters of their life together, concluding that his illusion of happiness only existed because of his child. It was time for him to let it go and move on, regardless of the hurt all of them would sustain in the process. Denise had found a man who made her happy. A man that helped her to forget she had a husband to begin with. In a way Jeff was glad she'd chosen to venture out. Her betrayal made the hardest decision of his life much easier.

The plaguing thoughts were too much for Jeff to stomach. Especially after six slices of cheese and hamburger pizza. He decided finally to turn off the light and let his daughter sleep in peace. Making his way into the master bedroom, he noticed more than just a couple of things out of place. Denise had come home and left. Did she really not believe she'd married a dumb mother-fucker? Or could she have cared less that he knew she was fucking another man behind his back? He could only make excuses for his wife's carelessness but, at the end of the day, it all amounted to one thing: she just didn't give a damn.

He scoped out their room from top to bottom the same way Bones and Agent Booth did when they investigated a crime scene. He could tell Denise had been in a hurry as he noted the strewn pieces of clothing he'd seen on her earlier that morning before he'd left for work, on the floor now. It was a late night date, tonight was. The kind of date that would have you running home to shower, change into a five-hundred-dollar dress from Neiman Marcus, and lie to your husband about working late, again. Jeff didn't buy the first lie three years ago when she ran it on him, so why in the hell would he fall for it tonight? He was curious for reasons he couldn't explain about this new cat who entertained his wife's late nights. He wanted to know what more was Denise doing for this man than she stopped and refused to do for him. Matter of fact, what was he doing for her that Jeff wasn't, because in Jeff's eyes, Denise didn't have one damn reason to be stepping out on him. They had the big house in the posh suburbs, the nice cars, and the *look* of happiness.

He'd done everything in his power to keep her happy and had forced things to work for the sake of their daughter. It was Denise who didn't compromise.

So for this new man she had in her life, what was it about him? What did he do for a living? What kind of car did he drive? Did he prefer his steak medium or well-done? Was it the pussy she gave him regularly that kept his interest? The weak-ass head jobs? Or was it both? Jeff wanted to know all those things. Most of all, he wanted to see the twenty-five-thousand-dollar watch this motherfucker was sporting. Ever since he'd come across February's bank statement, he'd been on guard about the money in their joint accounts. He recalled going online to view their recent and past transactions, becoming outraged by all of the money Denise had spent on new clothes and shoes at high-end places, just to impress the clown.

Jeff caught himself frowning in the double-rounded mirror above their headboard. Why was he so mad when he should have been thanking the man? "Fuck it," Jeff cursed aloud. Any last-minute regrets he thought he had got shoved down the "fuck it" aisle he was walking. He tried and that was all he could do. He couldn't take anymore. He was going to wait up tonight for Denise and tell her everything. Tonight, he would get it all off of his chest because he couldn't keep this inside any longer. He pulled a suitcase down from the upper shelf of their large walk-in closet and reluctantly started to pack.

10

*D*enise washed down roasted lobster, crab salad, brown butter asparagus, and macaroni casserole with a glass of Cabernet Sauvignon. If asked later about the meal at Hibiscus, she would give the chef five out of five stars and the wait staff would merit the same. Dinner was excellent, the wine superb, and most importantly, her handsome date couldn't keep his eyes off of her. Hibiscus was a trademark example of how everything was big in the Lone Star State. It was Denise's first time in the swanky, gargantuan, high-end restaurant. She'd heard remarkable things about the place but had never made the time to check it out for herself.

The moment she stepped through the doors her breath was nearly taken away by the rustic and dominating scenery. The tall arched ceilings, white plastered walls, and romantic lighting made her feel warm and welcomed as she eyed the modestly dressed couples, both young and old, huddling over a cornucopia of food choices served in surprisingly generous portions. Denise and her lover blended right in with the upper-class diners as their waiter showed them to their reserved table.

Denise gaped at the oversized chocolate brown leather booths that coordinated with the ultrasuede walls surrounding the dining area. She could still smell the wood-burning fireplace she'd spotted on her way out of the restroom, and since she'd ditched her panties in the trash purposely in anticipation for whatever spontaneous fun Greg had in mind, her pussy was like a magnet for the heated flames. She adjusted herself in the booth, her bare ass caressing the silk fabric of her new dress. Greg professed to her once before that he had an obsession for a woman in red, so Denise knew just the outfit that would do the trick. It took her shedding twelve pounds in order to fit into it and she still barely had breathing room, but so what, it was all for him. Her low-cut neckline revealed just the right amount of cleavage while the diamond necklace he'd bought for her last month, laid solo. Her curvaceous body invited spectators who puzzled themselves on how she'd managed to pull the look together so well. Her smooth Nubian legs drew in quite a bit of attention. They were the thickest, sexiest pair of legs in the restaurant and Greg and several other patrons acknowledged them as so.

Denise picked up the cloth napkin spread evenly over her lap and dabbed at the corners of her mouth. She hoped the cherry lip color she'd freshened up moments before dinner arrived, hadn't faded away and destroyed her modish finish.

"Care for dessert?" Greg asked Denise, looking forward to the chocolate crème brûlée. He ordered the same dinner dish every time. Candied pecan crusted mahi mahi, and for his vegetables, whipped sweet potatoes and fresh spinach. Cleared his plate every time.

Denise placed her napkin on the right side of her own half-eaten and abandoned plate, just as a staff member reappeared to clear the table. She couldn't eat anymore or she'd bust out of her clothes for sure. "I am stuffed. If I take another bite of anything else, I will explode," she said, laughing as her hair slid off her shoulders. Her straightened jet-black strands exposed an innate confidence about her sex appeal. Glancing at her bare finger reminded her of the missing two-karat wedding band she'd slipped off before meeting Greg tonight. Denise didn't feel any different with or without her ring, but she believed she owed Greg the respect of not flaunting her infidelities in his face. Besides that, she wanted him to see her for who she really was and not some negative image of a desperate housewife searching for discreet extramarital trysts. This was an unusual situation she found herself in, but deep down in the depths of her soul, Denise knew that her actions were justifiable. There was no mistake about her love for her husband. But over time, their passion for one another began to dissipate. She'd outgrown their relationship and the constant arguments, disagreements, sexual withdrawals, and habitual lies she found herself engaged in were all effects of the relationship's change in temperature. All the hiccups in the marriage had allowed her and Greg to develop something so special that not even her wedding vows could come between them.

Denise leaned forward, staring across at Greg's perfect physique. The broad shoulders and pumped chest made her pussy purr. He wore a solid black Giorgio Armani suit accessorized with platinum cufflinks bearing the initials G.A. His black shoes were buffed to a high shine. He looked every bit the part of the multi-millionaire he happened to be.

"So what is it you wanted to talk to me about?" Denise asked, remembering Greg's request for the dinner date. Her enticing smile locked into place as her gaze began to settle deep within his.

Greg shifted in his seat, pulled his shoulders back, cleared the doubt from his throat. He took a look around the restaurant, wanting to capture their last moment together. For he knew in his heart that Denise wouldn't accept the truth as it was. She was married, but so was he. It would never work between them. Their limited affair had run its course and Greg knew if he continued to see her under the current conditions, someone would eventually get hurt, and he did not want that someone to be his wife, Vivian. He positioned his mouth to speak the words that had plagued him all day, his focus returning to Denise's sparkling brown eyes, jewels on display between long and curly eyelashes.

"Denise, I want you to know that I appreciate everything you've done for me these past three years," he started out. "Your time, your energy, your love." He said the words with a convincing smile. "You've given all of that to me."

Denise reached across the table and took his left hand into hers. She gave it a short reassuring squeeze. She hoped this was the moment she had been waiting for. The moment where he was about to propose to her. She paced her breaths.

"You are everything that a man could ask for in a woman. You're beautiful, talented, independent, educated," he said, realizing he could go on for days.

Denise blinked back the fresh tears shaking in her eyes. She'd been told all of the remarkable things he was saying before, but it took a man of Greg's caliber to make her actually believe them.

Greg looked around the room, asking himself was this the right place and time. "Bear with me, baby," he said. "I'm trying to figure out how to say this." Unbeknownst to him, the words came out mumbled, although, in his mind, they sounded clear as a cloudless day.

"Just say it," Denise encouraged him in a soft, melodious tone.

Greg stopped altogether. Why couldn't he do this? Why was it so hard to just tell her the damn truth, the way he should have done the first day they met?

❖ ❖ ❖

He'd just been visiting the office building and was leaving from his lunch meeting with an old friend who'd recently relocated his growing firm to the downtown high-rise. Then he saw Denise walking through the main lobby and toward the elevator he was about to walk out of. He was comfortably dressed in a Dallas Cowboys T-shirt, blue jeans and tennis shoes, so he wasn't offended when she didn't even look in his direction. He remembered the entire thing as if it was yesterday. He was still trying to adjust to the idea of his wife moving to Connecticut to care for her ailing mother who suffered from Parkinson's Disease. Greg refused to make the move but encouraged Vivian to go. While Vivian managed to fly back and forth every other weekend, Greg still felt that the distance between them was starting to take a toll on their marriage. Seeing Denise that day helped him to forget how lonely he was.

Denise's feminine scent was a natural aphrodisiac that teased his manhood. Her hair was braided in tiny long braids bundled together and cramped in a sexy tight bun. He marveled over her from behind. Her fitted tweed jacket and skirt ensemble stretched nicely over her thick ass. As she pressed the button for her floor, he couldn't ignore the huge rock weighing down her left finger. She was married. But his only concern was if she was happy.

The toasted caramel-skinned, plus-sized, hourglass-shaped woman standing in front of him was too engulfed in her phone conversation to have noticed she was being stalked. As the elevator doors opened she stepped off and moved hastily to her destination. Greg exited as well. Her beauty entranced him as she walked and spoke with a rare sophistication into the silver Bluetooth hooked over her right earlobe. His wandering eyes followed her path into Platinum Crest Investments. He took an inconspicuous spot outside of the office and admired her through the thick glass as she collected a handful of papers from the lady behind the front desk. He waited until Denise was out of sight before he walked in to question the lady about her. He'd learned Denise was one of the owners of the company. He took a business card and called for financial advice. Not even two weeks later she had persuaded him to use her invaluable services. He then signed over a $2 million check to invest. It was the beginning of a three-year affair.

Greg's thoughts were sidelined once he saw the short Hispanic gentleman walking back toward their table. The waiter handed Greg and Denise a silver tray of warm moist towelettes and miniature peppermints.

"Here's your card, sir. And thank you, Mr. and Mrs. Adams, for dining with us tonight. It has been our pleasure to serve you." He smiled, bowed, and then walked back toward the front of the restaurant, a fifty-dollar tip in hand.

Denise smiled, loving being acknowledged as Mrs. Adams, even if she wasn't—yet.

Greg slid the Black Card back into his wallet. "What do you say we get out of here and go somewhere a bit more private?" he asked Denise.

Denise was immediately intrigued. "Sure. That's all right with me," she said. "Actually, since my car is still at the office, we can just go there."

That idea suited Greg just fine. "That works," he said, rising to his feet. He extended his hand for hers and they walked hand in hand through the assembling crowd, Denise's mid-length red dress moving fluidly with her curves. Once they arrived at Greg's car, he opened the door for her and she got in. He leaned down to kiss her, tasting the everlasting peppermint flavor on her breath and tongue. "I love you," she told him, in between their kiss. He hadn't expected her to say that. He was infatuated with the idea of loving her, but not being *in* love with her. Never had he realized how powerful those three words were when they were packaged together. *I love you.* It made him think harder. Longer. Could he continue to get away with this? And his wife. What if she found out? He couldn't imagine the financial ramifications if Vivian were to discover the affair and seek a divorce.

Greg finally closed Denise's door and walked around the rear of his vehicle to get to the other side. There had to be another way to handle this and he was going to figure it out soon. As for tonight, all he wanted was to block everything out of his mind, and he knew exactly what would help him do that.

Nadine had been at the office returning phone calls for well over two-and-a-half hours. She'd decided to go in and catch up on that day's work. Her desk was piled high with manila folders containing all of the clients' portfolios that she personally managed. A few of them had come by the office in her absence, and some had left voice messages regarding their financial concerns. Each of the messages reemphasized how the market was sliding and their investment money along with it, as if Nadine didn't keep up with Wall Street. They were all paranoid. They wanted out. Some even mentioned putting the leftovers into high quality bonds and treasuries. They wanted financial security. They wanted guarantees. They wanted a miracle to happen.

Nadine nearly fried her brain reading through literature for other alternatives to pulling completely out of the market. Because if that happened she couldn't recover her clients' losses. Not one red cent. She wondered what Denise thought about all of this. Surely her clients were worried, too. Over $50 million was at stake if less than half of their clients pulled out. Nadine knew how serious this was and how great of an impact it would have on their firm. She tried to come up with solutions that would persuade her clients that taking a walk wasn't in their best interests. But she came up empty.

Sipping from her strawberry soda, Nadine took a huge bite of the microwaved vegetarian pizza she'd somehow overcooked. The cheese topping was as brown as the crusted bottom but none of that mattered to her because she was starving. With one hand over her wireless mouse and the other occupying her late-night dinner, she ran her eyes over the stock market prediction chart. Things weren't looking up at all. In fact, the economic crisis was starting to scare her, too, as she read through the data on her screen. She reviewed several articles, even dabbled in a few of the ongoing conversations in a "money talks" members-only chat room where she saw the words recession and Great Depression so many times that it gave her a damn headache.

Overall, everybody was feeling the sting of the troubled economy. Paranoia had found its way all over the web as she read blog after blog after blog. Analysts and advisors offered their opinions but so did the victims who felt they'd been raped by the stock market. Anger and fear created ongoing discussions that convinced Nadine to log off of the internet completely. She had enough to deal with in the pile of paperwork before her.

Another full hour into her work, the fuzzy feeling in her stomach from earlier returned. Nadine nearly bounced out of her seat to jet for the ladies room. With one hand clutching her belly and the other her mouth, she rushed into the single stall. She squatted over the toilet, holding her bent knees, and puked out the cardboard pizza, strawberry soda, Twizzlers, and banana cream pie yogurt she'd eaten earlier. She closed her eyes, her chest pounding through her blue cotton spaghetti tank. She counted to ten, and just as she reached nine, she was doing it all over again. Vomiting. "Bghhhaa…" she retched.

Ten minutes later, Nadine flushed the toilet and sent the contents spinning down toward the sewer. She walked over to the sink and rinsed her mouth with cold water. She faced herself in the diamond-shaped, mounted mirror. Her eyes were puffier than normal and clammy skin replaced her natural glow. She looked sick and worn because all she'd done lately was eat, vomit, and sleep. Something was definitely going on with her but she didn't know what it could be. She'd heard on the news that another woman had died from the spreading swine flu virus and all she could hope was that the swine hadn't gotten a hold of her, too. Nadine felt her body becoming weaker and decided to call it a night and make it her business to see her doctor first thing in the morning.

Retreating back to her office, a woman's faint voice stopped her dead in her tracks as it echoed throughout the corridor. It startled Nadine at first, commanding her to stand there and listen. She waited. Nothing. She figured it was all in her head as she resumed her walk. "*Awww!*" the scream came again. Nadine's first instinct told her to run. That was before the sound got louder, stronger. She was so scared, she was shaking. She quietly ran for the kitchen break room. The voice sounded off again. This time she recognized it. She opened the closet door that she had at first contemplated hiding in, and grabbed the first thing she set her eyes on.

Holding the object the way a baseball player would hold a bat, Nadine followed the trumpet of sound.

11

Greg lifted Denise onto the edge of the conference table. With her Nubian legs spread and dangling at his side, he stepped in between them. The long wooden surface comfortably accommodated a total of twenty in one seating, but the only purpose he needed it for right now, was as a bed. As their tongues wrestled each other's, he eased both of his hands along her thighs. He squeezed them a little, and anxiously rolled up her dress to discover that she wasn't wearing any underwear. He was stimulated by the freaky idea of her eating, talking, and walking this entire time without any panties on. She wanted him so bad she took it out in public, naked. It reminded Greg of the parks, the lakes, the parking lots, and the hotel rooms where they'd often made out. They'd even had a couple of rounds in his Plano office. Sexually, they were married. Denise satisfied all his needs and wants. That was why telling her this wouldn't last forever was so damn hard.

Greg moved his hand between Denise's legs and circled her budding clit in a counterclockwise rhythm with his thumb. She wrapped her calves loosely around his back. Her melting pussy was dripping all over the table and she didn't care. It was *her* firm and *her* suite. That allowed her the privilege of having sex whenever and wherever she pleased.

Denise helped Greg down to his white T-shirt and it only took her one try to get his slacks undone. Her overflowing nectar made a pool between her legs. She let her head fall back as his middle finger moved effortlessly through her warm opening. It swam inside of her like a fish, but Denise had become too spoiled and accustomed to the real thing to settle for a substitute. "Make love to me," she whispered, her eyes drifting.

Greg pulled his finger out of her slowly, and with his own two eyes he witnessed how wet she could get for him. He could take a shower inside of her pussy. He brought her face closer to his, took his coated middle finger and proceeded to sculpt her lips with her own marinade.

Denise muffled a moan, forewarning him that she was beyond ready for all the freaky shit he might have had in mind. Greg leaned into her and sucked the sticky sauce right off her lips, then drove his tongue up and down her chin, her neck. It made Denise go wild. Made her beg and squeal and speak in a vernacular consistent with sweaty sex.

"It's your pussy, baby! All yours."

Greg reasoned that he would adopt her version of the story they told themselves while they performed their adulterous acts. That way they'd both have a mutual understanding. When they were together, it was always *his* pussy, and when they were apart, her goods were traded back to their rightful owner.

Greg lifted Denise's legs onto his shoulders, ready to medicate her. She wanted him to make love to her; according to her definition, the love had already been made. She was getting the best of both worlds. Whatever Denise wanted it to be, Greg was doing right now as his dick gave her pussy some exercise. He sexed her without a conscience. Without a doubt. It was his pussy she had told him, and that was all the approval he needed.

Denise couldn't hold it in any longer. It felt so good she had to let it out. "Awwww!" She gripped the corners of the table, her climaxes building one on top of the other. With every deep penetrating thrust, her pussy tightened around his dick. They were almost home, she could feel it. She nearly yanked her dress over her head, and tossed it behind her. Greg was mopping the floor with her pussy, knocking on her ceiling, and banging on her walls. "It's here. Right here," she said, losing control.

Greg reached to unsnap her bra, freeing her breasts. He hadn't been with a black woman since before Vivian, and Denise never failed to remind him of what he was missing as her chocolate titties added to his performance. Sweat trickled down the sides of his face but he refused to slow his pace. His name sounded so angelic on her tongue. He couldn't get enough of hearing it. Then he repeated in his mind what she'd told him all night, *It's your pussy.* He began violently shaking inside of her as his entourage battled over which direction to go. Her nails punctured the sweaty skin on his back as she gave birth to her most recent nut. With his shaft still hard and throbbing inside of her, he watched her make faces as she called out a woman's name.

"Nadine!"

Before Greg could turn around, he was receiving a powerful blow to his back.

Nadine beat the man with a long, skinny, umbrella until the metal handle broke off. She didn't hear her friend yelling at the top of her lungs for her to stop, and even if she had, she would have kept swinging.

Denise finally managed to snatch the umbrella out of Nadine's hands. She looked at her as if she was crazy. "Nadine, what the hell are you doing?" she screamed.

Greg struggled to his feet, oblivious to what had just happened. One moment he was diving in some good pussy and the next he was getting beat with what he thought was a bat. He hurried to take cover, his now soft dick exposed to the stranger that had just attacked him.

Astounded and in shock, Nadine stared the man down like an untamed dog, both fear and malice lurking in her unbelieving eyes. Then she recognized who he was. She'd seen him on several occasions. He was one of their clients. "I thought he was raping you!" she yelled back at Denise. "But apparently I was wrong." Her eyes went from Denise to the half-naked man in front of her. She was disgusted, to say the least.

Embarrassed by the awkward predicament she was in, Denise told Nadine, "I can explain this." She turned to Greg, an apologetic plea on her face. "I'm sorry, but I have to deal with this. Do you mind giving us some time alone?"

Greg quickly got dressed and began searching for his keys. "Don't worry," he said, his breathing labored. "Just call me." With that, he hurried past Nadine and out the door, telling himself he could have been killed here tonight.

Denise, still naked, reached for her bra and began dressing in front of her friend.

"So when were you going to tell me?" Nadine asked, her long face still petrified at what she just witnessed.

Denise eased the dress over her head and shoulders. "I was going to tell you earlier today. I just didn't know how," she explained, searching for her shoes. She hoped Nadine wouldn't comment on the fact that she hadn't seen her put on any underwear. She located her silver peep-toe pumps and strapped the chain around her ankles.

Nadine was furious now. "How long have you been cheating on Jeff?" she asked accusingly.

Denise almost didn't respond in the manner she knew was appropriate. She was so close to stepping outside of herself as a mouthful of curse words armed themselves for Nadine and whatever judgmental comments she was ready to shoot her down with. Denise took a deep breath, stood up after getting her shoes on, and answered her friend calmly. "Three years."

That literally knocked the breath out of Nadine. She shook her head. Jeff had been right about Denise. She was having an affair and he knew it. It was the same sixth sense that women were blessed with. He had come to her for advice that night, but she refused to believe that about her friend. She'd given Denise too much credit. She'd told Jeff that it was nothing. That the feelings in his gut were all wrong. And then what did she do? She fucked him to relieve his worries. Fucked him to justify what he knew his wife was doing behind his back. Looking back on it now, she hadn't done herself any favors. It was Denise that had benefited from everything while Nadine had only been a temporary replacement. Jeff had fucked her out of grief. Out of pain. Denise had made a buffoon out of her, warranting the poor judgment she used that night.

"I've tried to stop, but I can't," Denise continued. "I'm in love with Greg and he's in love with me. I really didn't mean for it to happen this way but Greg and I belong together. We're happy."

"I wonder if him being a millionaire has anything to do with it," Nadine lashed out. She knew Denise's taste. She was money and status driven. He fit the profile. "How many more of our clients are you fucking?"

"How dare you!" Denise stared Nadine up and down. "I didn't cheat on Jeff because I didn't love him, because I do. With all my heart. It just wasn't working for us anymore." Her confession came out without any remorse. Almost as if there was no real wrongdoing. She ran her fingers through her tousled hair. "That's it. End of story," she concluded.

Nadine didn't know if she should pick up what was left of the umbrella and hit Denise across the head with it a few times, or just hear her out and agree. But the more Denise talked the more Nadine didn't want to hear anything else she had to say, because all she could hear playing through her mind were Jeff's own words. *She's cheating on me.* Nadine stared at Denise as though she were contagious with some deadly disease. She felt rage rising inside of her and she knew exactly why. All this time she had been worried about Denise and her feelings when she should have been guarding her own. Denise didn't deserve Jeff. She never did. Nadine was sure of that now.

Denise saw the condescending look on Nadine's face. "So I suppose you're judging me now?" she said, squeezing out a mirthless chuckle.

"I'm fucking Jeff," Nadine blurted out of nowhere.

Denise went quiet. Her expression unchanged.

"Did you hear me? I said, I'm fucking your husband." Nadine's neck rolled as the words spilled out of her mouth and off her chest. "You don't deserve him. You never did," she added. "You've done nothing but lie to him. Including about Deandra being his." Nadine was sticking it to her where it hurt the most as her venom-laced words booby-trapped Denise. "Why don't you just be a real fucking woman for *one* day, Denise, and tell him that she's not his child so he can move on with his life? She's the only reason the two of you are still married."

Denise looked at Nadine with a straight face. "I'll tell him when I damn well please," she said, disregarding Nadine's confession.

"No! I'm not going to stand by another damn minute and watch you walk all over him."

Denise just shook her head. Nadine was in love with her husband. She was wearing the glow in her eyes. She was defending him. Denise leaned against the table she'd just waxed with her ass. She exhaled. This was her moment of truth. "You're right. You shouldn't just stand by and watch." Denise concealed a grin. "Although voyeurism can be so stimulating," she said, smiling.

Nadine stared at Denise as though she had lost her everlasting mind.

"Look, you want a confession. I'll give you a confession," Denise said. "I've always known about the affair with you and Jeff." She narrowed her eyes. "Who do you think orchestrated it?" She coolly asked the question. When Nadine didn't say anything, Denise guffawed. "Please tell me that you didn't think for one minute, I didn't know." Denise gasped. "Come on. You've always wanted Jeff. You think I never noticed the way the two of you look at each other? You really think I'm that fucking naïve?" She chuckled. "You just made it to where it was one less dick I had to suck," she retorted, cold as ice.

Nadine was shaking her head as tears welled in her eyes. "Why would you do this?" she managed between the tears.

"Because you didn't have the guts to! I practically shoved him into your arms, so you should be thanking me right about now, instead of judging me!"

"Thanking you? Are you serious?" Nadine questioned in disbelief. "You used me and dragged me into this sick, twisted game you call yourself playing—"

"I don't remember putting a gun to your head, Nadine. So you are just as sick and twisted as I am. I'm the one with a ring on her finger. Or did all the fucking you two were doing cause you to forget that?"

Nadine's head was spinning as Denise took her around in circles. She placed her sweaty palm over her forehead. "Why did you even marry him?"

"You know exactly why I married him. I did what I had to do.

I was not going to raise my child alone and without a father the way my mom had to do with me."

"That's not a real excuse," Nadine challenged, cutting her off before she could finish her sentence.

"Our marriage was over before it ever got started. You and I both know that." She paused. "It was built on a complete lie."

"It still wasn't fair to Jeff!" Nadine said.

Denise shot her a menacing look. "Since when in the hell is *life* fair? Do you think I asked to be raped that night? Do you? Deandra's biological father is a damn homeless crack addict and you're talking to me about fair! Please, spare me that sentimental bullshit!" Tears slowly began to skate down Denise's face. She covered her mouth and looked the other way.

There was a long, pregnant silence.

Nadine suffered from her own guilt, but learning for the first time that Denise was behind all of this burned her up inside. She'd been forced into a world of deceit with Jeff, and Denise was the puppeteer, pulling their every string. It infuriated Nadine. Forced her to look at Denise differently.

"I never meant to hurt Jeff. That wasn't my intentions," Denise admitted.

Nadine took a deep breath and began looking around the room. Neither of them said anything for a long moment.

"Are you in love with my husband?" Denise finally asked, breaking the silence.

Denise's question caught Nadine off-guard but she answered it the only way she knew how. "Yes. I'm in love with him," she declared.

Denise looked straight ahead, her emotions scrambled and unpredictable. "Well, I want you to keep seeing him."

"So you want me to just act as if none of this happened tonight?"

Denise took a deep breath, reached for her purse, and turned back to Nadine. "No. But I do want you to give me time to tell him about Deandra. And then, the two of you can go on with your happily-ever-after lives. "

"I don't understand the purpose for any of this," Nadine said.

"What's so hard about it? I'm granting your wish. You wanted my husband, and now you have him." With that, Denise turned to leave.

12

*G*reg eased open the Moroccan entry door of his cus-
tom brick and stucco mansion, hoping that his wife
was already asleep inside. As tonight's events played
episodically in his mind, he kept looking over his shoulder, fearful
someone was following him. He engaged every lock, including
the deadbolt, ashamed to consider the possibility that the only
thing haunting him like a Freddy Krueger nightmare was his
own conscience.

The house was as dark as the night that crept over it, surrounded
by four acres of manicured lawn and an exotic lake of teal blue
water. The gated property's subdivision was secured by a two-
man team that provided him with the peace of mind he needed
at times like this when he felt physically drained and defenseless.
The stone menhirs outside and the free-standing figurines adorned
throughout the inside of his house were beginning to look like
tiny foot soldiers as he stared at them. He closed and opened his
eyes. He was making himself delusional.

He moved in a disoriented gait across the hardwood floors,
through the foyer, and down the elongated hallway toward the
west wing of the house. He tried to brush the scent of his girl-
friend off his clothes until he figured simply removing the jacket
and shirt would be much smarter and less detectable. He decided
that he would toss everything in the laundry and tell Vivian, if

she asked, that he'd had a couple of drinks with friends. Things had gotten crazy. Beer spilled and so on. He'd make up the rest of the lie as it came to him. He'd tell her whatever she needed to hear to shut her up.

He stopped at their bedroom door, the smell of gardenia seeped through the cracks, while the lyrics of John Mayer described how Vivian must have felt on the other side of the door. Greg walked into their bedroom and was greeted by his wife. She was half-naked, in white lingerie and white pumps, lying across the black bedspread. Her long sandy-blonde tresses, now in loose curls, draped her bare shoulders. A long pearl necklace hung down to her belly button, matching a similar pair of pearls that adorned her ears. Greg glanced over at the tray beside her, undressing himself while taking in the scenery. Plump red strawberries covered in chocolate lay on the tray. A bottle of 1995 Krug Clos Ambonnay Brut champagne chilled in an ice bucket.

"I wore this on our honeymoon," Vivian said as she measured the surprised look in her husband's eyes. "Remember?"

Greg was speechless. He wondered what had gotten into Vivian. Why the sudden desire for intimacy? "I'm going to shower," he said before walking casually into the bathroom. He stripped down to nothing, burying the clothes that reeked of Denise's scent in the pile of dirty laundry in the closet. Then he remembered that Vivian had given the maids the week off. He couldn't imagine doing his own laundry, and hopefully Vivian wouldn't get the urge either, so leaving the clothes in the closet was a risk he had to take. Infidelity had left him open to many such risks.

Vivian patiently waited for him to come out of the bathroom, even though he hadn't responded in the manner she'd hoped for. But the new therapist she had been seeing all week warned her of this. She had also told her to be patient with the process and that Greg was grieving in his own way. The woman had told Vivian a lot of things, but still she wanted tonight to be every bit of perfect. Just the way they were three years ago before her mother got sick. To make it so, she'd gone to the salon and spent over three hundred dollars on her hair and makeup. She realized how distant and selfish she'd been. How she had completely abandoned her marriage. Nothing would bring her mother back and she couldn't keep taking her anger out on her husband. Greg didn't deserve to be left behind while she moved to Connecticut. He deserved better than she'd given him since her return, too. She understood this now. Their marriage was important to her, and she was going to work very hard to get things back to the way they used to be.

Greg wiped the fogged bathroom mirror with the towel he'd just dried off with. So many thoughts ran through his mind; he couldn't process them all. He wondered if Denise had made it home safely. He wanted to call and check on her but decided it would be best to wait until morning. He walked back into the bedroom, the heavy gray towel hanging on him by a loose tuck.

Vivian's face lit up. She picked up the tray and pushed back the sheets so that he could climb in next to her.

"Not tonight, Vivian," he said.

"What do you mean, not tonight?" Working to distance herself from the shock of his words, she reminded him, "Honey, it's been months."

"Six months to be exact," he said matter-of-factly. He didn't feel like arguing. "I'm just not in the mood tonight." Spoken calmly, without him raising his voice. He turned off the lamp on his side of the bed and closed his tired eyes. "Tomorrow I should feel better."

Vivian didn't know what that was supposed to mean. She stared at Greg's backside in disbelief. After some time she slowly lifted herself from the bed, blowing out the trio of candles arranged throughout the room. She turned off the music and scooped the tray into her hands and walked with it to the kitchen. Tears streaked her face as she moved to the wet bar, drinking glass after glass of Scotch over ice chips. She cried and drank herself into a mental frenzy. As the concoction of fluids began taking advantage of her body, she started to feel like the alcoholic her mother had been. Infuriated, she threw her empty glass where it crashed into a wall. It sounded no louder than a pen dropping in the cavernous house. She cried into the wee hours of the night about things beyond her control. Things she was certain of and even things she wasn't certain of. She wished she could call her father and share with him how much she missed her mother. He'd cry with her. He'd tell her everything was going to be okay. They'd relive every single memory as if her mother was still there with them.

Another glass found its way into her unsteady hand. She lit up a cigarette and smoked and drank until her body grew even more numb.

Two hours passed and Vivian lay down helplessly on the hardwood floor, curled in the fetal position. She thought she was dying. Thought it was the end of her world. More tears came and the feeling of dying went away as her lids sheltered the whites of her blue eyes.

13

"And where the hell have you been all night?" Jeff confronted Denise the second her eyes opened. He was fully dressed for work. Normally she was up before him, but today she still slumbered in bed with slobber crusted on the side of her mouth. Or was it some nigga's nut? Jeff wondered. In actuality, he didn't really give a damn anymore. Still, he expected to be treated with some level of respect and decency.

"What time is it?" Denise asked groggily, rising from the bed.

"Mommy!" Deandra came flying into the room. "I need you to sign my paper for the field trip."

"All right, sweetie," Denise said, trying to wake up all the way. "You're all ready for school, I see."

"Daddy let me get ready all by myself," Deandra said cheerfully. She had on her navy blue school uniform and white blouse underneath. She wore her white tennis shoes with white socks. She was so proud of herself.

Denise only smiled. Her daughter's pigtails were lopsided and her barrettes were backward. "Give Mommy a kiss," she said, pulling Deandra into her arms and hugging her tight.

Jeff just watched as he collected the last bit of things that he needed to load into his car. "Let Mommy and Daddy talk for a second," he told Deandra.

Deandra looked up at her father and left without pause. Besides, her cartoons were on.

Jeff waited until his daughter was out of the room and far enough away that she couldn't hear what he was about to say. He closed the bedroom door.

Denise braced herself as she stared up at her husband. She thought about the conversation she'd had with Nadine last night. She wondered if Nadine had spoken to Jeff about their discussion. But even if she had, Denise was okay. She had prepared herself for the worst. The fact still stood that she was in love with someone else that shared her interests, her mind, her aspirations. Greg was on her level and was already where she wished she was in life. He had status. All Jeff had was potential, and for Denise that just wasn't enough.

"What's on your mind, Jeff?" she said, ready to get it over with. She felt it would simplify things if he just said his peace and kept it moving. No need for drawn out speeches when they both knew what time it was.

"I'm going to camp out at a friend's house for the next couple of weeks," Jeff said. "Just until I get some things off my mind."

Are you kidding me? He couldn't even look her in the face and tell her the truth. *So he wants to punk out*, she thought. But she was going to make this easier for the both of them. "A friend?" she asked, getting out of the bed and walking over to where he was. "Does this friend have a pussy and go by the name of Nadine?"

Jeff felt as though the air had just been knocked out of him. He swallowed the lump in his throat and looked everywhere but at Denise.

"What, cat got your tongue?" she asked.

The cat had more than his tongue right then. It had his balls too. "Look, Denise—"

"No! Don't 'look, Denise' me. Nadine is my friend!" she yelled, spraying his face with spittle. "Out of all the bitches in the world, `you had to fuck *my* friend! My business partner." She lashed out, turning this all on him. It was easier this way, she reasoned.

Jeff was too scared to even breathe. The look in Denise's eyes spoke of murder and he did not want to end up on *48 Hours*, the victim of a crime of passion. He looked at Denise, broken by the sight of her wet eyes. "I'm sorry," was all he could muster.

Denise deserved an Oscar for her performance. "Yeah, you're sorry all right," she said, shaking her head. "You're sorry that I busted your cheating ass!"

"Now wait a *got damn* minute!" Jeff had to catch himself. He brought his voice back down. "I was going to tell you, had you given me the chance."

"Oh yeah? When?" Denise asked, throwing her hands on her wide hips.

Jeff wanted to tell her he'd began cheating because he suspected that she had been stepping out on him. But he knew that wouldn't lessen the hurt he'd caused by having an affair with her best friend. He wished Denise hadn't found out before he'd had the opportunity to tell her, but he was relieved that she finally knew. "I'm going to just give us time apart so we can decide on what we need to do."

"What is there to decide on, Jeff? You leave, I keep the house. I paid for it," she reminded him.

Jeff's face settled into a frown. Denise often acted as if he didn't contribute to anything they had together.

"My furniture. My car." She went on to name everything she'd paid for. "So the decision has been made for you."

Jeff saw it coming as clear as the bright blue sky. She was so damn materialistic. She could have every damn thing in here because he didn't want it anyway. She was correct about that. Everything was hers. She bought it with her own money while all his money went straight to fucking bills. "You can keep all this," he agreed. "What we need to discuss is my daughter."

Denise felt her heart shudder. She didn't want it to come out this way, but Nadine was right, it was time he knew. "Jeff, Deandra's not yours."

He squinted his eyes and bit his bottom lip until he drew blood. "What did you just say?"

"I lied to you," Denise confessed. "There. So now you have it."

Jeff closed his eyes and balled his fists. He felt his breathing escalate.

"I didn't want it to come out like this," she said. "But it's time you knew the truth."

Everything Denise had just said went unheard as Jeff reached for her neck. He squeezed until her eyes watered. Until she gagged. Until the color left her face. Her life was in the palm of his hands.

Breathing hard as beads of sweat collected on his forehead, Jeff slowly released his hold, sending Denise into a coughing fit. She grabbed for her throat as she bent over, trying to catch her breath.

Jeff felt as if his heart was bleeding like an open gunshot wound. He swallowed his pride and allowed a solo tear to creep down the side of his face.

With her hand on her chest, Denise stood to her feet. She witnessed the pain in Jeff's eyes and regretted telling him this way. She had never seen her husband cry in all the years they'd been married. Nor had he ever laid a finger on her. Tears rolled down her face as well. "I didn't cheat on you," she tried to explain. "I was raped! I just didn't know how to tell you."

Jeff remained silent.

"You will always be her father," Denise said, moving closer to him.

Jeff backed away, shaking his head and cursing her to Hell in his mind. "Stay the hell away from me!" He slid off his wedding band and dropped it on the floor. "I'll be back later to get the rest of my things," he said before walking out of the room.

"Daddy, Daddy, are you taking me to school?" Deandra called out as Jeff zoomed right past her. "Mommy, where's Daddy going?" Deandra asked, confused as she turned to her mother who was walking toward her like a zombie. "He's leaving without me and I'm going to be late for school." If she was late she wouldn't receive a gold star for the week, which would cause her to lose out on extra playtime at gym. Seeing that her mother wasn't even dressed or paying her any attention, Deandra spoke louder, practically yelling. "Daddy left me, Mommy!" She bucked her knees, a frown on her face. "I can't be late for class."

"He's leaving us." Denise began to cry as it finally sank in for her. What had she done? "I don't think he's coming back," she told Deandra.

Deandra cried with her mom, only she didn't understand why her mother was telling her that her father wasn't coming back. More tears burned her eyes as snot ran from her nose. She no longer cared about the gold star that she wouldn't be receiving. She wanted her father. "I want Daddy!"

Denise embraced her daughter. "It's okay, baby," she said, rocking her in her arms. "Everything's going to be just fine." Only she didn't believe her own lie.

14

"Well, I have good news!" Dr. Switz said, walking back into his office where Nadine waited patiently on the green suede chaise.

Nadine straightened her posture.

"You don't have the swine flu," her doctor continued.

Nadine's face lit up with surprise and instant relief. She exhaled. "That's great news. I was so worried."

"Well, I don't want the two of you to worry too much," he said. "You need to take it easy, starting right now."

Nadine frowned. "What did you just say?"

"Yes. You heard me right," Dr. Switz confirmed for her. He looked over her charts, taking a seat in the swivel chair behind him. "According to my calculations, you're about fourteen weeks along. Give or take a week."

Nadine said nothing but her puffy eyes were almost the size of golf balls. She was delirious. The small private room seemed to cave in, suffocating her. Her stomach twisted in tight knots. "I can't be pregnant," she said, shaking her head in complete disbelief.

Judging by Nadine's reaction, Dr. Switz concluded that this wasn't a planned pregnancy. And although he had known Nadine since she was three years old, that didn't mean he knew what turns and shortcuts she expected to take in life. His theory was, if you were a woman having sex without protection, expect to have a baby! It was that simple for him, but the female patients who came to him for wellness exams once their bellies had already started to swell didn't quite understand that logic. And just about every one of them thought they had a stomach tumor. Today, it was the swine flu. He'd seen and heard it all.

Dr. Switz forced himself to be as sensitive as possible while maintaining his professionalism. "Will you be going through this alone, Nadine?"

Nadine lifted her head and looked at her doctor. She had the answer in her mind but her lips wouldn't fix themselves to utter it. "This can't be happening to me. The test has to be wrong. Please. Let me retake it. I'm sure they made a mistake with mine."

"Nadine, just calm yourself and let's take a seat right back here." He walked her over to the chaise. Dr. Switz didn't want her to get worked up. "Nadine, I can assure you we have the correct results, but for you, I'll have the nurse administer the test again."

Nadine was slipping into a daze. She felt light-headed. "Thank you, doctor."

"One more thing. Here's a card of a very good OB/GYN. She'll get you started on your prenatal vitamins and will monitor you through your entire pregnancy."

Nadine hesitantly accepted the card. As light as she knew the card was, it might as well have weighed a ton. She looked it over with glossy eyes that made her vision blur. The red letters against the white cardstock stood out boldly.

"You'll love her," Dr. Switz added.

Nadine didn't respond. Her mind was set on not being pregnant. She couldn't bring a child into this world knowing the wrong circumstances of how it was conceived. "I'm not pregnant." She stood, forcing the card back into her doctor's hands. "So, I won't need this."

"Ms. Collins, please."

She slapped at her jeans. "Where's the cup? I need to get this over with."

Dr. Switz grinded his dentures. "Follow me, dear." He had nothing more to say.

Nadine sat in the Starbucks parking lot across the street from the Lexus dealership debating on whether or not she should go over there. She asked herself if Jeff's workplace was the best place to tell him that he was going to be a daddy. It took Dr. Switz allowing her to retake the test, and Dr. Gene confirming a second positive result, for Nadine to believe that a tiny life was growing inside of her. All of this time she'd figured it was all the stress that had caused her periods to stop.

There was an instant love Nadine felt for her baby. A love she had never quite given to anyone before. Nadine was overwhelmed with joy and sadness. The combination discombobulated her thoughts until she was only a short breath away from having another asthma attack. She inhaled, then exhaled. Everything was happening too fast.

Taking a healthy sip of her Chai tea, Nadine let the mingling flavors mollify her. She considered picking up the phone to call Jeff instead of just popping in on him. Either way, this wasn't going to be easy. She'd gauge his mood, and if it was pleasant then she'd walk right in his office and tell him face to face that she was carrying his seed. Just as she dug her right hand into her purse to retrieve her cell phone... *Tap, tap, tap!* The knock on her window was startling. The hot tea she had in her other hand spilled all over her. "Awwww!" She rolled down her window in disgust.

"I'm so sorry, miss. I hate to bother you."

Then don't, Nadine thought. *I'm emotionally occupied.* "Yes?" she quipped, an irritated smile on her face.

"I just missed my bus. Can I borrow your phone to call my job, please? I need to tell them that I'm going to be late."

Nadine looked down at her white shirt. Brown stains were splattered like paint all over her. She took a deep breath, then handed him her phone. He didn't take long making his call and while Nadine was somewhat nervous, she knew he'd be stupid to try anything with her. She had a full can of pepper spray she wasn't afraid to use.

"Thank you, ma'am. Oh…" The man reached into his pocket and pulled out a ten-dollar bill, handing it to Nadine. "Sorry about the coffee. Have two on me." With that, he turned and walked back to the bus bench.

Nadine stepped out of her car and walked back into the café. She headed toward the main counter. Her shirt was ruined, now she had to go all the way back home and change. She stepped back in the line. A young man, nicely dressed, with long wavy hair stood in front of her. He ordered a black coffee with three shots. She thought about Jeff. That was his exact recipe for a daily start. The cashier asked for the name to call on once his drink was ready.

"Canvas," he told her.

Nadine liked that name. It was unique. Then her thoughts went back to her baby. She had to figure out what she would name him or her. The idea of being a mommy was starting to win her over as she found herself smiling. But then again, did she really want to do this alone?

Canvas stepped out of line, slinging a black duffle bag over his right shoulder. Nadine proceeded to place her order for the second time that morning. Coincidentally, everything was starting to happen in doubles. Once her name was called, she took her tea, holding it tight, then headed home to change clothes, once again.

15

*J*eff drove eleven miles out on the interstate and inadvertently passed the exit for the dealership. He was zoned out from the rest of the world and in a state of mind where he could have killed somebody. That somebody was his wife. He hated the thought of her, the smell of her, and the visual she'd left him with as she tore him down, bit by bit. Denise had walked all over his pride, pissed on his feelings, and shitted on his heart.

Jeff exited the highway and circled his way back around, wondering if Denise had ever loved him. If she ever cared. It was clear they had married for all the wrong reasons, but was there ever any love? Jeff intentionally ignored his ringing cell phone, unwilling to have his train of thinking interrupted. He just wanted to be left alone right now. That was the best thing for him until he figured out how he would deal with everything. He pulled into the dealership, parked in the rear next to Janene's SUV. He waited in his car, listening to the radio for twenty-five minutes before getting out.

A great amount of laughter carried throughout the building as Jeff walked inside. He headed straight for his office, hoping to go unnoticed. His plan failed miserably when Stacy Harrington, his general office clerk, spotted him and called out his name.

"Mr. Jackson!" Stacy ran over to her boss. "You had me worried sick. Your wife has called numerous times this morning looking for you. She said it was urgent. Is everything okay?"

Jeff raised both of his hands, then shook his head. "If she calls again, tell her I'm out of the office for the rest of the day," he said firmly, adding, "Please," after realizing how bossy his directives sounded.

Stacy stared at him bug-eyed. She wanted the scoop. The details. "All right. I'll be sure to let her know." She hurriedly turned around to look for Kim, Janene, or Chelsey, the offices' biggest gossips, hoping they knew the juice. She could smell the drama cooking after only being out for two days on sick leave. She couldn't wait to get the low-down on everything that happened while she was gone.

Jeff turned the door handle and let himself inside of the privacy of his own domain. There was so much shit on his mind he knew he'd never be able to concentrate on work, so why did he even bother showing up? Then that reason walked right in the door.

"Mr. Jackson, you look like you could use one of these, sir," Canvas said, carrying a tall cup of black triple espresso over to him.

Jeff studied Canvas. He hardly recognized the boy in his pressed gray suit and blue tie. The few facial hairs he did have were neatly trimmed and his hair was slicked back into a single plait.

Steam rose to the top of the cup and filtered throughout the office. Jeff brought his chin up, then desperately took a sip. "Hmm. I see you've done your homework."

Canvas smiled. "You can say that."

"You're early," Jeff noted, looking down at his watch.

"I realize that, sir. My grandma used to say to me that the early bird catches the worm, and with public transportation, you'd be late to your own funeral. So, I wasn't taking a chance. I caught the early bus."

Jeff chuckled at the grandma's wit. The boy was proactive. Jeff liked that in a worker. "Well, since you're already here, I see no sense in waiting. So let's get started."

Canvas took a seat in the same chair he'd sat in yesterday, only today he was sure he'd leave with a new job. He could feel it. He flattened his tie over his chest, pinned back his shoulders, then folded his hands out in front of him.

Jeff recognized the confidence in Canvas, but how long would that confidence last? He'd seen the best of the best break under pressure. He'd seen some of the top salesmen walk through the door and leave in less than a month because they underestimated their competition. So as he studied Canvas, he wondered where he would fit in. The boy was only seventeen. What could he possibly know about sales?

"School. Are you going?" Jeff asked, taking another swig of his soothing hot morning beverage.

"Yes, sir. Faithfully. I'm a senior and I have all my credits so I only have one class a day."

"I see," Jeff said. He leaned forward in his chair. Canvas seemed to be very relaxed and sure of himself. He decided he'd throw him the curveball from yesterday. "Canvas, why should I hire you? What can you bring to my team?"

Canvas had prepared himself all night for this. "Well, Mr. Jackson, I'm a hardworking young man. I'm talented, energetic, and I make great conversation. Oh, and I can sell the shirt off your back," he added with a smile.

He is just as cocky as I once was, Jeff thought. "Okay. Well, we'll see about all that." After a series of questions, Jeff picked up the phone and dialed Miss Janene's extension. "May I see you for just a second, please?"

Miss Janene, a twenty-plus-year employee of the dealership, appeared in Jeff's doorway in a matter of minutes. "Yes, Mr. Jackson?"

"Could you show Mr. Canvas Green around and introduce

him to the rest of the staff? I'll get his paperwork started, but since he's so anxious to get to work, you can get him started on that project we talked about in our last sales meeting," Jeff hinted.

Miss Janene nodded her head, smiled, and then turned to Canvas. She extended her hand. "Pleased to meet you, Canvas. I'm Janene. Everyone calls me Miss Janene. You'll see me moving a little slow around here but don't pay me no attention."

Canvas stood to his feet. "Nice to meet you, ma'am. By the way, I love that fragrance you're wearing," he said, smiling.

Miss Janene blushed at his compliment. "Why, thank you, Canvas." She liked him already.

Jeff stood from his chair. "Congratulations." He extended his hand to Canvas. "I admire your ambition. But it doesn't stop there."

"I won't let you down, sir," Canvas said, reading between the lines.

"Good."

Canvas followed Miss Janene outside to begin his first day of work.

Jeff spent the morning hours on the Internet looking up information about paternity tests. So engrossed he worked past his lunch hour without realizing it. He wanted to be certain that Deandra wasn't his biological child, regardless of what Denise said. He wanted the truth for himself. Besides, he saw himself in Deandra from head to toe. She had his ears, his mouth, even his thick jet black hair. She had to be his. She had to. There was a double knock at his door. "Come in," he called out.

"Mr. Jackson," Chelsey began, "there's a Nadine Collins here to see you."

Jeff was baffled. He wasn't expecting her. "Thank you. Go ahead and send her in." He began clearing his desk, glancing every so often at his daughter's picture on the screensaver as he did so.

Nadine walked in, smiling. She was wearing a burnt orange maxi dress and brown open-toed sandals that showed off a fresh pedicure. Her hair flowed evenly over her shoulders and her makeup was subtle yet effective.

"Good afternoon," Nadine greeted, shutting the door behind her so they could talk in private. Nadine didn't mind the snickering or the odd looks she felt when she asked the door greeter where she could find Jeff Jackson. She had even recognized one of the women who cackled as a parishioner from her church.

Jeff looked down at his watch. It was eleven minutes past one o' clock. "Hey, you," he said, trying to appear calm despite the jolt of Nadine popping up unannounced. He leaned over and planted a kiss on her lips. "To what do I owe this pleasant surprise?"

"I just wanted to see you. I've missed you," Nadine said, taking a seat as he did the same. "Have you not gotten any of my messages?"

Jeff was hoping she wouldn't ask that. "I haven't had time to check the voicemail," he admitted.

Her face fell into a frown. "So you haven't missed me enough to pick up the phone and call?" A wide range of speculation shadowed her thoughts. They'd committed to never doing that very thing to one another. Jeff had promised Nadine that he would never make her feel left out, or alone, and now she found herself questioning those sentiments. Her emotions were scattered by everything that had transpired last night, on top of what she had learned today. The last thing she needed was for Jeff to be as distant as he was. "I'm starting to feel like you don't love me anymore," she said. "Like I'm not a priority in your life." Jeff was quiet, not responding fast enough for Nadine's liking. Why did she have to express herself this way when he should have already known?

He stood up and walked around his desk, closer to her. He did not have the clear mind to deal with any of this right now, and he was smart enough to realize it. He didn't even know how to respond or how he should feel. He couldn't even reach far enough in his heart to know that the motherfucker was still beating. Yet she expected an honest answer, when all he could offer her was an excuse. It seemed that overnight their relationship had come to a standstill and Jeff accepted that.

"We said we wouldn't do this," Nadine continued.

Hearing Nadine talk about her feelings, helped Jeff to notice that she had misinterpreted everything all wrong. By not calling he hadn't meant to make her feel less important or secondary— although she knew second was exactly where she fit into his life. He hadn't called because he needed space to clear his head. Besides, it had only been one day.

"I guess you just didn't miss me enough," Nadine continued, rambling.

"Baby, of course I missed you," Jeff said, pacifying her feelings long enough for her to look at him and reestablish their connection. "I'm just going through some things right now and I don't want to take my frustrations out on you. That's all." Jeff felt a tightness in his head and all he could do was shake it off and let out an exasperated breath.

"Is it Denise?" Nadine asked.

Jeff looked away for a moment, then brought his attention back to Nadine. "Yeah," he answered shortly.

Nadine exhaled, an uneasiness settled all over her body. She already knew where this was going and she was already sick of hearing about it before he had even started. She wondered what lie Denise had filled his head with this time.

"Nadine," he said. "Denise and I are getting a divorce."

Nadine blinked her eyes a few times as if what he was telling her wasn't registering. "Divorce?" she asked, her brows furrowed.

Jeff gave himself a moment before he responded. He never thought he'd be in a situation like this. "It's over between us. I'm moving out."

A part of Nadine wanted to jump up and down and parade all over the desk but she didn't. It wasn't appropriate nor was it tasteful. Instead of feeling as if a victory had been won, a sense of sadness washed over her. She felt guilty knowing she had contributed to their failing marriage. "I'm sorry," she managed, looking Jeff in the eye.

Jeff walked away, not wanting Nadine to see the sadness filling in his eyes. He balled his hands into two tight fists, wishing he could ram them through the glass window. Maybe then he'd feel better. "There's nothing to be sorry for," he said to Nadine. "She lied to me."

Nadine listened. She waited for Jeff to fill her in on everything he knew before she volunteered the inevitable.

"How could she just lie to me like that?" he asked.

Nadine rushed over to her lover. "It's okay, baby. I'm here," she consoled, taking his hands into hers. He closed his eyes, tilting his head back as his teeth bit into his bottom lip. Nadine figured that Denise must have come clean with him about Greg. She wrapped herself into Jeff's big arms. Maybe being caught in the act last night had helped Denise to discern that she couldn't keep getting away with this. She couldn't keep lying to Jeff and expecting that he wasn't going to ever find out.

"I was good to her," Jeff said, re-opening his teary eyes.

Nadine did know how good Jeff was to Denise. She knew better than Denise. "Jeff, you did everything right. Denise didn't realize the value of a good man like you," she said, hoping to comfort him. She messed up. She hurt you." Nadine's feelings took over from there. "And I don't want to see you hurt anymore." A tear slid down her face as she cuffed Jeff's chin in her hand.

"She never cared enough about how I felt. She used me!" Jeff lashed out in anger.

Nadine wanted to tell him that Denise had used both of them, but she didn't. "Calm down, baby," she said, taking his hand.

"Why did she have to lie about Deandra being mine?" he blurted. "She could have told me the truth. For all she knew, I would have still took her in. Why did she have to make a fool out of me?"

Nadine lifted her head. It seemed as if church bells were ringing in her ears. Her voice held hostage by her own indiscretions.

Jeff stopped talking long enough for her to get her words together. But even with the moment of pause, Nadine still didn't know how to say what Jeff was entitled to hear.

"Just tell me one thing, Nadine," he said. His eyes were blood-shot and rimmed with bags because of a lack of sleep. He could barely keep them open, even with all the caffeine swimming through his system. "Did you know that Deandra wasn't mine?" Her hand slipped completely out of his as the question hung there in the air.

Nadine found herself in a crossfire. On one side there was her best friend for over ten years, and on the other, Jeff, her lover, her friend, and now the father of her own child. Her speech was choppy as she tried to explain. "I. She. There was no way I could..." she went on, losing her words along the way.

"So are you trying to tell me that you knew Deandra wasn't my child!" Jeff shouted. "And you didn't tell me?"

"Jeff, please. Let me explain," Nadine begged.

Jeff looked at Nadine as if she had inflicted the worst pain upon him. He shook his head. Barely breathing. "I can't believe you."

"I wanted to tell you, I just—"

"But you didn't!"

"I didn't want to—"

"What? Betray her?" Jeff spat coldly. "You weren't thinking about all that while we were fucking! Or are you fucking my wife, too, because apparently you cared more about her being hurt than you did me?"

Nadine couldn't believe him. Tears covered her face. "Jeff, stop it!" She had never seen him like this.

"You know what," Jeff said, rubbing his temple. "The best thing for you to do is leave me alone right now." He took a few deep breaths.

"No. I'm going to stay right here and we're going to talk about this," Nadine cried.

Jeff focused his incredulous eyes on Nadine. Through gritted teeth, "I trusted you."

"You still can."

"You made a complete fool out of me. All this time...and I actually was starting to believe we had something special."

"We do." Nadine's eyes pleaded with his. "I'm telling you that I can explain all of this."

"What is there to explain? You knew from day one Deandra wasn't mine. That's why this shit hurts! Day fucking one, Nadine. You're no better than my no-good-cheating-ass wife."

"You don't mean that. I'm everything that she's not," Nadine managed despite the tears clogging her throat. "Just give me a chance." She reached for his hand and he jerked it away. "Jeff?"

"Do I look like I'm playing games with you?" He walked back over to his desk, grabbing his jacket. "I don't ever want to see you again." He reached into a desk drawer and pulled out his car keys. "Let yourself out."

"Jeff!" Nadine called out. "Please. Don't do this to me! I can't do this alone. I can't."

Jeff closed the door in her face. As he made it to the front of the showcase center, he called over the intercom for Canvas.

Canvas hurried to the sales floor. "Yes, sir?"

"You hungry?"

"Hungry? Man, I'm starvin' like Marvin," Canvas said, wiping the sweat from his brow after being out in the heat peeling old sticker tags off the marked-down inventory.

Jeff saw the door to his office slowly open. Nadine was still crying but no part of him cared long enough to even acknowledge her pain. "Come on. Lunch is on me," he said to Canvas before turning his back on Nadine.

16

Nearly four-and-a-half weeks had gone by and Denise hadn't heard one word from Jeff. She didn't know whether he was dead or alive; he seemed to have vanished from the universe. She couldn't believe he didn't have enough consideration to call and tell her where he'd be staying, follow-up by letting her know that he was doing okay, or at the very least an angry call to let her know he wouldn't ever talk to her again. She found herself worrying constantly, hoping that he would one day find it in his heart to forgive her. She hated how things had turned out for them, but she knew that it was all for the best. She loved her husband, but the problem was that she found herself loving Greg more.

To resist further complicating things, Denise had asked Greg if they could have a cooling period. Understandably, he agreed. He made her feel so important when he told her that he wanted to give her space and time to go through the healing process. Said he knew how difficult of a time it must be for her and her daughter.

Denise used the weeks of her separation from Jeff to accomplish some important things. She had already sought out a divorce attorney, hoping to finalize the dissolution of the marriage without stepping a foot in court. That was something she wished to avoid at all costs. She was also hoping to settle their personal matters like two civilized individuals who cared about the welfare of their child.

Denise had a lot of thinking to do but she couldn't keep her thoughts from the perfect future she painted in her mind with Greg. She knew how selfish it was to donate the time to that thought, but Jeff had moved on, so why shouldn't she? Even with Greg's concerns that she focus first on healing herself, Denise knew the healing wouldn't begin until she was back in his arms and back making sweet love to him over and over again. Though for now, she took herself through the motions, ready to speed things along so that she could get back to living her life. She didn't want Greg to inherit any of the stress that was momentarily dragging alongside of her. So she'd recover, move on, and start a brand new life, with a brand new man, without anything standing in their way. And the best part of it all was that Greg couldn't wait to meet Deandra.

Denise poured herself a glass of ice-cold water as everyone filed into the Mosaic room one at a time. It was the largest of three conference rooms she and Nadine used for their meetings. Denise placed the pitcher back on the table and then took a sip to wet her parched mouth. She lowered the glass once a smiling Nadine entered the room. All eyes were on Denise's partner for some strange reason, and everyone in the room besides Denise, gave Nadine a hug. Denise placed her glass on the plastic coaster, more than ready to start the meeting.

"All right, thank you all for being here. On time," she said, smiling. She received a few chuckles from her staff, then cleared her throat and hit the light switch to dim the room. She pushed one button on the table and a long, flat, projection screen descended from the ceiling, becoming everyone's primary focus.

Nadine slowly made her way to the front, by Denise, occupied the first seat she laid eyes on, grabbing for a jelly doughnut as she settled in.

Denise didn't say a word to her counterpart, just began her presentation.

"During the quarter's end, Platinum Crest Investments funded $12.2 million to existing portfolio companies and received $7.6 million in repayments."

Nadine bit into her doughnut, savoring every bite until it was all gone. Her mind was everywhere but in the meeting.

Denise pressed a button on the remote and changed the slide.

"The weighted average yield on targeted portfolio investments was 6.58% at March 31. The weighted average yield on investments in corporate notes was 5.82%. On investments in U.S Treasury Bills and cash equivalents, 0.13% and 0.31%, respectively. The weighted average yield on Platinum Crest's total capital invested was 6.05%."

Denise took another sip of her water and moved to the next slide.

"The primary cause of the decline in the weighted average yield on targeted portfolio investments as of March 31, is that the calculation includes a negative yield on our investment in the ATP Oil & Gas Corporation limited term royalty." Denise picked up the copies of her PowerPoint presentation and began passing them down the row. "These cost basis figures are outlined on these spreadsheets," she stated.

Nadine squinted her eyes, reviewing the data in front of her. Although the loss they took was astronomical, business was still thriving according to the report. She had worried herself all for nothing.

"As you can see, the yield is the result of amortization on the investment being significantly higher than the revenue earned for the month, this is due to a decrease in oil and natural gas prices. In addition, though the investment is substantially hedged and such hedges produced substantial income for the month of March, such income is not included in the yield calculation for targeted portfolio investments as the investment in commodity hedges is not included in the targeted investment portfolio. Further, we continue to maintain our investments in Formidable, BSR Loco Bayou, and Chroma Exploration & Production, Inc. on non-accrual status."

Everyone turned to the front of the room as the door hinges squeaked. "Mrs. Jackson, there's a lady here to see you," Tonya announced.

Denise looked at Tonya as if she was disturbing a prayer service. "Can you tell her that I'm in a very important meeting?" she asked nicely.

"I did. She's insisting that she speak with you."

Denise took a deep breath. "All right. Nadine, will you, please?"

Nadine stood as Denise handed her the remote. She didn't know where to begin because according to these charts, her own calculations were off by a mile. She had thought they'd taken a much bigger hit than what Denise revealed.

Denise followed Tonya down the hall.

"I tried to tell her that you were in a very important meeting but she really didn't seem to care," Tonya told her boss. "She said it was an urgent business matter."

As Denise and Tonya headed to the front, a tall white woman with long silky black hair, stood patiently. "Good morning," Denise greeted her, wondering what the woman could have wanted with her. She surely didn't look like someone interested in doing business with Platinum Crest.

"Ma'am, are you Denise Jackson?" the woman asked.

"I am."

The woman extended a plain white legal-sized envelope. "I'm Cynthia Monfort, process server for the state of Texas. You've just been served," she stated clearly.

As the woman walked out of the office, Tonya's eyes followed her curiously. She wandered over to Denise as her boss tore at the envelope with her nails. "What is it?" Tonya asked, resting her hands on her indiscernible hips.

Denise pulled out the documents. It was a court summons. She began reading the first sheet over. Her eyes rested on the word PATERNITY. She couldn't believe Jeff didn't have the balls to call her and tell her he was taking her to court. Why would he put Deandra through this? *Got damn him*! She shoved the papers back in the envelope, forcing a smile. "It's just a summons for court," she told Tonya. "One of our clients seems to be in some legal trouble again," she lied nervously.

"Oh," Tonya said, relieved. She walked back to her desk and sat down, flipped through the last few pages of the maternity catalog she'd borrowed from Nadine the day before.

"Shopping again?" Denise asked, changing the subject. She didn't need her staff in her business.

"I wish," Tonya said. "Girl, you know that wedding knocked us back forty grand. Lee's still trying to recover." She laughed. "I'm just catalog browsing for when Lee and I do get something in the oven. Nadine must be very excited."

Denise walked over to Tonya as the secretary folded the catalog and placed it inside her desk. "Are you telling me Nadine is pregnant?" Denise's eyes showed her surprise.

"Yeah. Haven't you noticed that flat belly of hers getting bigger? Besides, she finally broke down and told everybody after we kept teasing her about all those jelly doughnuts she's been eating. She's keeping Emma in business with the way she eats those things religiously." There was a brief pause before Tonya said, "Wait. You didn't know?"

Denise allowed the thought to linger. "You know, it's coming back now. She did tell me." She let out a convincing chuckle. "Why, where is my head? I guess with everything that's been going on, it just slipped my mind."

Tonya shook her head. "You need a vacation. Either that, or you're getting old," she said, laughing. "And doesn't somebody have a birthday coming up?"

"Hey. Now see that's a whole month from now so please, let's not rush it," Denise said.

"All right," Tonya said, pretending to surrender. "Not another word from me. Ha, ha, ha. Until next month."

"Bye, girl. I have a meeting to tend to," Denise said playfully.

"Okay. I promise not to interrupt again," Tonya called out as Denise hit the corner. She picked up the ringing phone. "Platinum Crest Investments, Tonya speaking."

Instead of going back to the conference room, Denise made a beeline straight for the restroom. Alone, she leaned over the basin and allowed the mirror to witness her pain. A twinge of jealousy crept over her as the idea of her best friend being pregnant by Jeff settled in. She thought about how devastating this would be for Deandra if her daughter discovered the truth. Denise couldn't take it. She placed her hand over her heart. It had no rhythm. Her entire body felt paralyzed as she played devil's advocate in her mind. The pain she felt couldn't express itself, even in her reflection. She couldn't cry because this was what she had asked for. It was what she had created and that was the reality of all this. She straightened her clothes, took a deep breath, and walked back out the door.

"Platinum Crest is still a leading investment firm with over $9.6 billion of cumulative capital under management since inception, serving all sectors of the energy industry," Nadine concluded. She met eyes with every sitting person in the room. "Does anyone have any questions?"

No one said anything, only shook their heads no.

"All right. Class dismissed," she said, smiling, taking a seat while everyone cleared the room. Nadine didn't know if it was the baby that always made her feel tired, or if she was simply getting too fat. She couldn't take one step without feeling shortness of breath. She rubbed her belly.

"So you didn't think I should know?" Denise asked.

"About what?"

"Your situation."

Nadine's eyes smiled at Denise. "You seem to know everything. I was sure you read the memo before I ever sent it."

"Funny," Denise said, pressing her lips together. "So how does Jeff feel about it?"

Nadine stood to her feet, whispered through clenched jaws, "I'm not about to have this conversation with you. We are in a place of business."

Denise shut the conference room door and walked over to where the woman whom she'd once called a friend stood with Jeff's firstborn inside of her. She shook her head. "Okay. Well, then, since you can't answer that for me, here's another one." She crossed her arms over one another. "Have *you* told Jeff yet?" she charged.

"I will."

"Humph," Denise scoffed. She had figured that much. She wondered how Jeff would react to Nadine's delaying the news. Wondered if he would choke the shit out of her until she nearly passed out, like he had done her. "Well, that's none of my business so it hardly matters. But if I find out that you had anything to do with this." Denise whipped out the court summons and held it in the air. "You will curse the day that you opened your legs and got involved in *my* marriage."

Nadine twisted her face. "Are you threatening me?"

Denise didn't bother answering the question. A smile so sinister crept over her face she didn't need words to escort it. Nadine could take it however she wanted as long as she understood the language coming out of Denise's mouth. Denise rolled her eyes, opened the door and walked out of the room.

Nadine followed behind, heading in the opposite direction. She walked quickly toward her office, collected a few things that she could carry in her hands, and put them in a separate pile from everything else she packed. She phoned one of the interns and he came rushing into her office. Jim helped her box tons of files, asking questions the entire time while Nadine ignored them all. When they were done, he took the files back to his office to sort through, just as Nadine had asked.

Nadine's desk was almost naked with only a pen and tape dispenser. All her files had been moved to Jim's office and all her emails forwarded to Tonya for Denise to distribute. She grabbed her cardigan, shut her door, and walked out of Platinum Crest Investments with no intentions of ever coming back. Denise would have her email resignation of partnership by morning and the signed hard copy the next day via FedEx. She was going to make it through this one way or the other. There was a flutter in her belly. She had to. This wasn't just about her anymore.

enise lay across her mother's bed feeling sorry for herself. She hadn't slept a wink since the letter came to the office four weeks and six days ago. Why was Jeff doing this? She knew in her heart that Nadine must be behind it. Denise's understanding attitude apparently wasn't enough. *"Well, I want you to keep seeing him,"* she had told Nadine. But Nadine wanted more. What should have remained between the three of them now involved Deandra as well. Denise sobbed into a pillow. How was she going to tell her baby that Jeff wasn't really her father? That Mommy had lied to the both of them. How would Deandra ever forgive her?

"Honey, are you okay in here?" Grace asked, walking into her bedroom. Denise and Deandra had stayed over for the past three nights, preparing for today.

"Yeah, Ma. I'm fine," Denise lied.

Grace sat beside Denise on the bed. She had never seen her daughter so broken and she hated seeing her this way. "Everything's going to be okay," she promised, rubbing Denise's shoulder.

Denise knew her mother well enough to know that she was lying to her in the nicest way possible. There was nothing that could fix this. "Does he even want to be in her life anymore?" Denise asked her mother. "He hasn't called or even come by to see her. It's not Deandra's fault, Ma. I did this to them!"

"Shhhh. Shhhh." Grace rocked Denise in her arms. Although she believed that Denise was wrong for deceiving Jeff, she perfectly understood Denise's reason for doing so. But Grace wasn't one to take sides. She loved her son-in-law, and no matter what happened between Jeff and Denise, he would always be a part of the family. Just as Grace was about to divulge her own secret, Deandra walked into the room.

"Hey, Mommy. Can I go outside?"

Denise wiped her eyes. "Yeah, baby. Stay on the front porch, though. And we're about to leave in a few more minutes so don't get anything on your clothes."

"Okay," Deandra said, running for the front door.

"And stop all that running!" Grace yelled after her.

Denise pulled herself up from the bed. She was catching hell at both home and work. Nadine had resigned as partner and the legalities of the broken partnership drained Denise just as much as the drama in her personal life. She was so damn stressed. And now she had to deal with Jeff dragging her into court for something they could have taken care of in the privacy of their own home. To make matters worse, Greg hadn't returned any of her phone calls. She knew he was a busy man but the least he could have done was make time to call her. Denise left message after message, day and night, all for nothing. She didn't know what to make of it. She began resenting Jeff and Nadine all the more. While her life was in shambles, they were out planning their future together as a new family.

Denise sighed deeply. It felt like karma was coming back around to settle a score. Denise reached for the nightstand and grabbed the bottle of Tylenol. The past few weeks she'd been waking up to headaches. She popped two pills into her mouth and swallowed them down with water, dragged her feet out of the bed and stood up to walk across the room, her body feeling weaker with every step.

Grace's gaze followed her daughter. She hated seeing her this way. Depressed and out of it. She hoped what she was about to tell her would relieve some of those burdening worries.

"Denise," she said. "Jeff hasn't forgotten about Deandra. He's been coming by the house every single day since the two of you split up." Denise looked at her mother, wide-eyed.

"He's been coming by to see her?" Denise repeated weakly.

Grace nodded her head. "Yes."

"Humph. And you didn't think I should know that?"

"I promised Jeff that I wouldn't say anything," Grace said. "He didn't know how you would react. Besides, that man is hurting as much as you are right now. And when he came by here yesterday after Deandra got out of school, he looked so stressed."

"Fuck him. I'm your daughter!" Denise reminded her mother, raising her tone. "How could you sit here and lie to me when you knew that every single day I waited for a phone call from him. And the both of you had Deandra lying to me, too."

"No! Now you wait a damn minute," Grace spoke up. "We didn't ask Deandra to lie. Matter of fact, we didn't ask Deandra to keep anything from you. But that child ain't stupid! Don't you think she knows something's going on?"

"No. She doesn't know anything and I would appreciate it if it stayed that way," Denise said, cutting her mother a menacing glare.

"Well, she's gonna learn about all this mess sooner or later. And then what you gonna say? You lie to her now, and you'll regret having to face her with the truth when she's older. She'll hate you for it." Grace caught her breath. "You can't possibly believe that keeping her in the dark is the best thing for her."

Denise rolled her eyes. It was time to gather up Deandra and leave. She began putting their things into the mini suitcase. "I will raise my daughter how I want to raise her," she said. "If Jeff wants to remain a part of her life, great! If he doesn't, that's fine with me, too. But regardless, I'll raise her *my* way."

Grace walked closer to Denise. She was two inches shorter than her daughter. Despite that she stood tall and looked Denise in the eyes. "So you think you got it all figured out, huh?"

Denise stuffed the last few items in the bag and zipped it.

Denise was just as stubborn as her mother and Grace took ownership of that. "Jeff means well. He's just trying to digest everything, chile. Respect the man's decision on that."

"You know, Ma, you sure do have such good things to say about Jeff. He means well, he wants to be in Deandra's life, he's hurting, he's this, he's that..." Denise carried on. "What else did he tell you? Seeing how the two of you make so much time to discuss me and my daughter. Well, did he tell you the real reason we're getting a divorce?" She waited for her mother to reply.

Grace plugged her ears. "I have no interest in hearing that," she said. "It's none of my business."

"Did he tell you he was having an affair with Nadine behind my back?" Denise said louder.

Grace's mouth flew open and her hands fell to her sides.

"Yeah, I didn't think so. Your sweet son-in-law isn't so sweet after all, now is he?" Denise said. She stopped what she was doing and let her head fall back. Who was she fooling? She had caused all of this. Nobody but her. But it was easier to handle all of this when she made herself believe that she was innocent and that she was the victim.

Grace walked over to Denise and placed her hands on both sides of her daughter's face. "It's going to be okay."

Grace took her thumb and wiped at the tears falling from Denise's eyes.

"I can't believe I'm standing here crying," Denise said, nearly laughing at the absurdity of her reaction.

Grace gave her daughter a confused look.

Denise slipped into her flats, suitcase in hand. "I'll call you after the hearing," she said, shutting off her tears all at once. She gave her mother a quick kiss on the cheek and started for the front.

Grace's long purple housecoat swept the floor as she followed Denise to the living room. Denise opened the screen door and as if they'd seen a ghost, the two of them stood frozen in their tracks.

"Happy birthday," Jeff said. Deandra was in front of him, beaming up at her mother.

"You're a day late," Denise retorted, ignoring her daughter's bright smile.

"Better late than never."

Frowning, Denise eyed her husband peculiarly. "What are you doing here?"

"I came to see my daughter. Our daughter," he corrected, squeezing Deandra's shoulders.

Deandra stood closely in front of her father.

Grace reached her hand out for Deandra's. "Come with me, baby. Grandma's got something pretty she wants you to see."

Deandra took Grace's hand and followed her into the back of the house.

"Okay, so now that you've seen her, why are you still here?" Denise's words came out hostile. "Being how she and I are due in court in the next forty-five minutes, we're pressed for time."

"Okay. Well. I was also hoping that I could talk to you for a second."

"We're talking."

"Stop. Please. Let me get this out," he pleaded.

Denise looked at her watch. "You have ten minutes."

"It'll only take me five."

18

*D*enise sat on her mother's blue-and-burgundy living room couch, wearing the most disgusted look on her face. While it would be impossible for her to ever stop loving Jeff, at that very moment, she despised him for dragging her and Deandra to court. "I can't believe you're doing this to me," she said the second he took the seat beside her.

"To you?" Jeff fired back. "So you think my wanting a paternity test is about you?"

"Deandra did not have to know about this," she said. "You are way out of line for involving a child in adult matters."

"I only told her we weren't on speaking terms because I felt she needed to know the truth as to why I don't live with both of you anymore," Jeff said, matching Denise's volume.

"Well, you were wrong!" Denise said through clenched teeth. "My job as her mother is to protect her feelings."

"By lying to her, like you did to me?"

"I had to lie!" Denise shouted. "Had I told you the truth, you wouldn't have believed me!"

"It doesn't take a genius to figure this out, Denise. You cheated on me and then tried to trap me with your mistake—"

"You're calling my baby a mistake?" Denise said, getting up from the couch. "You son-of-a-bitch. Just get out! Get...out!" More tears streamed down her face, ruining her makeup.

As soon as he'd said them, Jeff wished he could take back the words. They'd come out completely wrong. "I'm sorry," he said.

"Sorry is right," Denise fumed.

Enough was enough. Jeff couldn't handle Denise's misplaced anger any longer.

"I love that child in there. I raised her!" Jeff said, double slapping his chest. "I stepped up to the *got damn* plate and dropped out of college so that I could work and provide for her. But nah, I don't get any credit for that. I get punished for doing what I thought was right!"

"Did I ask you to fucking drop out? Did I? No, I didn't. So don't act like I'm the fucking reason your dreams didn't come true."

Jeff felt like he was being punched in the face. That's how hard and powerful his wife's words were. "You have a lot of nerve," he said.

"Look! Your five minutes are up. Now I'm going to give you this blood test but don't you ever discuss *our* business with Deandra again." Denise grabbed her suitcase and hollered for Deandra. "You ready, sweetheart?" she asked when Deandra appeared in the doorway, now dressed in one of the pink and white dresses her grandmother had made for her. Denise had braided Deandra's hair the night before in a long French braid that stopped right at her neckline. A pink and white ribbon was tied to the end.

"Say bye to your father so we can go," Denise said, walking out of the door and to her car.

"Bye, Daddy," Deandra said sadly.

Jeff looked at his baby girl while trying to shield the pain in his eyes. "Aren't you forgetting something?"

He squatted.

Deandra wrapped her arms around his neck.

"You'll always be Daddy's little angel, you know that, right?"

Deandra nodded her head, sniffling at the same time.

Jeff kissed her forehead and hugged her like he never wanted to let go. For the past few weeks all he thought about was the outcome of today's test. He wanted the results to be in his favor and he held on to that bucket of hope, faithfully.

Grace walked back in the room. "Your mama's calling you, baby."

Deandra withdrew her hold and walked beside her grandmother toward the front door. She waved goodbye to her father and headed to her mother's car.

Jeff stood and reached in his pocket for his ringing cell phone. He took one look at the name and sent the call straight to voice-mail. It was Nadine. She had been calling him every single day, and not only did he not want to speak to her, he didn't want to have anything more to do with her than he did his wife. Soon enough, he told himself, he would make sure she knew that. Jeff felt as if he had been a part of a nine-year scandal, and he didn't trust either of them anymore.

As the engine hum of Denise's black Chrysler 300 faded, a symbol of the growing distance between them, Jeff finally walked out of the house.

Grace sat on the porch in her favorite chair, staring into thin air, her Bible right beside her. "You okay?" she asked Jeff.

"I'm about as well as to be expected of a man who's about to find out if the child he's been raising for nine years is his." That was the last thing Jeff said as he walked down the sidewalk and got into his car.

Denise walked through the revolving doors of the downtown George L. Allen, Sr. Court building with Deandra by her side.

Although she knew what the outcome of today would be, her heart still raced as though she didn't. But the fact of the matter was there was absolutely no chance that Jeff could be Deandra's biological father. Because the day that Denise learned she was three weeks' pregnant, calculated back to the day that she was raped, she and Jeff had yet to have sex. So not only was she a rape victim, but she would have to live with and face that reminder for the rest of her life.

Two-and-a-half weeks after her sex-filled nights with Jeff began, Denise told him that she was pregnant. Jeff never even questioned it, even though he had never gone without strapping up. But Denise had gone as far as poking holes in his condoms so they would break in the midst of them having sex.

She had only confided in Nadine, and her best friend tried to convince her to abort the pregnancy, but Denise had made up her mind that she was not murdering her child. She believed that's what abortion was. Nadine then pleaded with her to come clean with Jeff but Denise refused, telling Nadine that she was not going to raise a child without a father as her mother had done with her. While Nadine disagreed with what Denise was doing, she swore to never tell a living soul, and she had kept that promise.

Denise slid her purse off her shoulder and placed it on the black conveyor belt. The burly white security guard standing behind the metal detector motioned with his finger for her to walk through. She met eyes with the second guard monitoring the assembly line of purses and briefcases that were rolling through on the belt. She was sure he recognized her from the past few times she had been summoned to court.

"Good morning," he greeted her.

Denise kindly returned the gesture. "Good morning," she replied with a weak smile. She snatched her lipstick-red Fendi tote off the belt and grabbed Deandra's hand, heading for the bank of elevators. Dressed in a navy blue pantsuit and flats, Denise moved quickly through the assembling crowd. She checked her watch again. She was ten minutes late. As soon as the elevator door opened, she got on. As she went to select her floor she saw that it was already lit. She took a deep breath and placed her hands on Deandra's shoulders. The second the door opened, she got off and started down the hall looking for the room number listed on her paperwork. She glanced down at Deandra who hadn't said a word since they'd left Grace's house. Denise was uncertain if her daughter believed the story she had given her on their way to the court but she hoped she had. She had explained to Deandra that they were having an ordinary dental exam. She even went as far as to describe the swabbing process.

Once Denise came to the room she was looking for, they went inside. She handed the woman at the front desk her court order.

"I'm Denise Jackson and this is my daughter, Deandra. We're here for testing," she said

"May I see your ID, please?" the woman asked, looking up at Denise over the spectacles that rested on the bridge of her nose.

Denise handed the woman her driver's license and after a series of questions, she and Deandra were shown to a private room. "Someone will be right with you," she said.

"Thank you." Denise looked around the room and wished that she and Deandra didn't have to be here. She needed to be at the office working and Deandra needed to be at school, learning. She shifted her attention to Deandra. "You haven't said one word to me. Are you okay?"

Deandra glared at her mother.

"Talk to me, baby. You know you can talk to me," Denise insisted.

"I wanna live with Daddy," Deandra said.

Denise placed her hands over her trembling lips as tears began to swell in her eyes. "Why do you want to live with Daddy, baby?"

"Because I miss him."

Denise tightened her lips and let the tears dancing in her eyes cascade down her cheeks. She forced what appeared to Deandra to be a smile when, in actuality, it was just a mask to hide her pain. Denise walked over to her daughter. "I'm so sorry," she repeated over and over, kissing the top of her head. "And one day when you're a lot older, you will know the truth. And I hope that when that day comes, you'll find it in your heart to forgive me." Her last words were barely above a whisper.

19

This was the day that Nadine finally found the strength to admit to herself that she had fucked up. Big time. She and Denise were no longer friends, and Jeff didn't want shit else to do with her, making his feelings perfectly clear by not returning any of her calls. He'd even let his voicemail fill up to the max so that now when she called there wasn't even the option to leave a message. She'd visited him at work the last day they spoke to tell him she was expecting. Never in her life was she prepared to tell him to his face that she knew Deandra wasn't his child. She cursed silently as a solo tear slipped from her right eye. She owed Jeff the truth but her battle was far more complicated than that. How could she be completely loyal to her lover when his wife had been her best friend? She thought she was doing the right thing. Thought she was staying out of *that* part of their marriage.

Nadine laid her head back against the soft mini-pillow she had brought from home and concentrated on the voice screaming in her head. *Three years you've waited on this man, only to fuck up now!* The voice continued to scold her. Nadine wasn't sure what she was going to do now. This condition of indecision led her to the one person that could help her solve her problems: Her Aunt Mickey. She had been planning to visit her aunt anyway, but after all of her drama unfolded, she decided to leave sooner. She needed to get away and clear her head before she had a mental breakdown.

The turbulence jolted her out of her thoughts. She opened her eyes and took one look around to see who was awake and who wasn't. Nadine's neighbor had been snoring the entire time, but with all the madness taking up residence in her mind, his snores sounded softer than a baby's coo.

Nadine drew in an exasperated breath, stretched her legs, and laid her uncombed head against the pillow again. She wondered if everyone else on the plane was running away as she was. Running away from the mistakes in their lives. Their drama. Love. And all the other bullshit that fell in between. This was harder than she thought it would be. Matter of fact, now that Jeff's baby was growing inside of her, it was almost unbearable. She missed Jeff so much she drove herself crazy from the mere idea of never seeing him again. She had considered getting an abortion, believing that would alleviate her problems, but when she had called for details about the procedure the counselor informed her that she was too far along. Now, her only option was adoption.

Nadine looked out of her neighbor's window. Somewhere out there somebody had been through what she was going through. She wanted to ask them how long it would take for her heart to stop hurting. As that final thought resonated in her mind, she drifted off to an unpeaceful sleep.

20

*J*eff stared at the result of the paternity statement over and over again that clarified that he was not Deandra's biological father. His head was still throbbing from the first time he read it earlier that morning. He had asked that his mail be sent to the office because that's where he spent all of his time nowadays. The stuffy one bedroom he was renting reminded him of his college dorm, but it was all he needed. Somewhere to lay his head at night. He was a simple man. Always had been and always would be. He shifted his gaze from the document when his office door opened.

"Mr. Jackson, I'm going to head on out for the night," Miss Janene said.

Jeff didn't realize how late it was. "Go ahead, Miss Janene. I'll see you in the morning."

Miss Janene's eyebrows rose. "Tomorrow's Sunday, Mr. Jackson. We're closed."

Jeff smiled. "Oh yeah, that's right. Well, then I'll see you the day after that."

Miss Janene was concerned. She had never seen her boss like this, but rumors had spread like wildfire all over the church about what had happened. Nadine and Denise had stopped going to choir rehearsal and Miss Janene couldn't remember the last time she'd seen Jeff on a Sunday. "So you won't be making it to church tomorrow?" she asked.

"I'm afraid not. But pray for me," he said, smiling. "Because it seems like God has been answering everybody's prayers but mine."

Miss Janene nodded her head and quickly closed the door before he could see her reaction.

Jeff checked the time on his computer. It was fifteen minutes past ten. He didn't know where he would go but one thing he knew for damn sure was that he wasn't going home. He turned off the office lights, locked his door, and set the alarm for the building. There was only one thing that he was sure would take his mind off everything, and as he climbed in his car, he headed straight there.

Jeff pulled into the crowded parking lot of a newly remodeled gentlemen's club, which was formerly a restaurant. He drove past the souped-up vehicles and found a parking spot in the far back. Still dressed in suit and tie, he walked inside the crowded hot spot. It had been forever since he stepped foot in a strip joint but this was exactly what he needed to take his mind off of his fucked up reality. Maybe a few rounds of Hennessy and a fine, horny hottie could help him cope with what he alone could not. Jeff paid the eleven-dollar admission fee and started for the back of the club, a serious swag in his walk.

The entire club was painted in hot pink with highlights of silver. There were floor-to-ceiling mirrors throughout and even the seven stages were chromed out with sparkling stones that looked like diamonds. The booths were adorned with pink fur and had cushioned chocolate brown leather seats inside. It was like something in a rap video, Jeff thought, as he peeped the scenery and the activities going on all around him.

The music was loud and there were naked women dancing or walking in every direction. Black women, Latin, Caucasian, and Asian. He was in every man's heaven.

Before Jeff could sit down and get comfortable, one of the dancers walked right over, introducing herself as Ménage. "You're a newbie," she said, outing him.

"Damn, is it that obvious?" Jeff chuckled. His eyes strolled up and down her fine, gold-dusted body, which shimmered underneath the minimal lighting. Ménage was at least five-eight, one hundred and thirty pounds, thick in all the right places. She was a butter-pecan brown with tight eyes, straight white teeth, and full luscious lips. But Jeff's attention wasn't on her pretty face, it was on her decorated twins. Her breasts were hugged together, sitting perfectly on her chest. It was too early for him to have those thoughts running through his mind, but he couldn't help it, they were there. He wanted to make love to her right here in the club. No wait, retract that, he didn't want to make *love*, he just wanted to fuck! Fuck her like his sanity depended on it. Jeff believed that he needed to take his anger out on someone, something, just as long as he was in control.

Ménage's long jet-black hair hung off her right shoulder and when she moved her head slightly to the left, the vision he had before him disappeared. Jeff looked back up and, for the first time, he noticed that she had hazel eyes.

"You need a drink to loosen up. So your first one is on me," Ménage said, smiling.

"You showing a brother love this early?" he asked, competing with the rap music.

"Yeah, I'm showing you love." She smiled and walked away.

Jeff's eyes took another trip roaming the club. Each of the lit stages was stripper occupied. Some of the women worked solo shows while the others tag teamed in an effort to double or even triple their money.

"Here you go, baby," Ménage said, returning with a full glass of Patrón. While Jeff might have thought he was getting special treatment, it was merely an investment. Ménage ran her fingers down the sides of his clean shaven face. She looked down at his finger and didn't see the wedding ring she expected. But wanting to personalize his experience, she asked anyway. Her aim was to get to know as much about him as he would let her. That was how she kept them coming. That was how she maintained regulars who wouldn't see anyone but her.

"Let me guess," she started. "Unhappily married or happily divorced."

"Damn. You're good." He smiled. "Separated. Pending divorce." He licked his lips, took a sip of his drink, and immediately felt the need to come out of his tie and jacket. The burn of the Patrón tickled his throat but he welcomed it. Feeling more comfortable, he brought his attention back to Ménage, who was sexily rocking her hips to an R. Kelly throwback. He leaned back and took another swig from his drink, his eyes still entranced by her erotic body. She moved like a belly dancer in front of him, making love to the music while he explored the possibilities. Jeff needed something to take the edge off. Something to make him forget about Denise, Nadine, and those fucked up paternity results. His concentration shifted to Ménage and her incredible hourglass figure. Ménage showed off her infamous tongue skills by making it curve under her chin. Jeff's member was growing inside of his pants but instead of groping himself to calm it down, he shifted in the booth and took another drink. The drink slowly began to work him over as Ménage seduced him. It was a terrible concoction but Jeff wanted it anyway.

Ménage did a slow wind and then slid her hands over her round apple bottom. She bent all the way over and touched her toes, showing off her flexibility. She made her ass clap, then made it bounce to the beat of the music, one cheek at a time. She slapped her booty and made it vibrate as she watched Jeff's expression from between her oiled and smooth, toned legs. He was in a pure daze and on an X-Rated high. His eyes were on her but his mind seemed to be in a million other places. Ménage stood up straight on her pink seven-inch Barbie stilettos and then climbed on top of the small round bar table that was directly in front of her customer. She laid back just enough to keep from falling and then spread her legs into an upside down Chinese split.

"I like to give my customers something to think about when they go home." She smiled seductively and spread her legs wide, allowing Jeff a good look at her hairless pussy. As he watched, she eased one finger, then another, inside of her dripping canal.

Jeff knocked down the rest of his drink and signaled for the half-naked waitress that wore pink-and-silver to match the color scheme of the club. She was over accessorized with as much costume jewelry bling as some of the ballers going in and out of the VIP room.

"Patrón," Jeff said without looking up at her when she asked for his order. His fixation had been on Ménage and all the freaky shit she was doing for him.

As Ménage finger-fucked herself real slow, she mouthed to Jeff, "You wanna taste some of this pussy, daddy?"

Jeff didn't even realize that he was nodding his head. It was as if he were under hypnosis or a voodoo spell. As soon as the waitress sat his drink down in front of him, Ménage eased her two saturated fingers into Jeff's drink. With her enticing eyes, watching his reaction, she stirred his drink with her fingers before pulling them back out and feeding them to him.

Jeff didn't even question if he was breaking club rules, that's how bad Ménage had him gone. He sucked his mixed drink right off her slender fingers one at a time, with the same gentleness and dedication that he wanted to eat her pussy. He couldn't help or control the feeling washing over him.

For the first time in the two months that Ménage worked at X-Rated, her customer had made her extremely wet. Once her fingers were licked completely clean, she went back to her exotic performance. When the song was over, she slid off her makeshift stage and looked at him as though he knew the drill. Seeing that Jeff wasn't catching on, she announced, "Table dances are forty," and waited for her pay.

As soon as she said it, Jeff realized that he hadn't been tipping. He pulled out his wallet and opened it. All he had was two twenty dollar bills and three ones. "Damn," he said.

Ménage rolled her eyes so that he couldn't see her. "What's wrong, daddy?"

"I didn't plan on coming here so I didn't bring any extra cash."

Ménage gave him a sinister smile, then pointed to the indoor ATM. "They'll make change for you at the bar."

Jeff got up from his relaxed position and headed straight for the ATM. He cursed under his breath when he saw that the transaction fee was six dollars, but he withdrew the cash anyway. He walked over to the bar. "My man, let me get some ones for this." He laid three hundred dollars in twenties on the counter.

The bartender swept the money in his hands and counted it. "This all I got for ya." He chuckled and handed Jeff a bundle of ones and the other two hundred dollars in fives and tens.

Jeff shook his head. "Of course that's all you would have," he mumbled under his breath, scooping the money up. When he returned to his seat Ménage was right there waiting. "Here you go, sexy." The exhilaration of what was to come flowed through him as he handed her fifty dollars in all tens.

Menage accepted the money, folded it, and slipped it into the tiny black pouch secured around her left wrist. "Now where were we?" she asked seductively.

Jeff finished off his drink and then waved the same waitress from earlier his way. He pulled his credit card out and one of the twenty dollar bills. He placed them both on her tray. "Keep 'em coming," he said.

"No problem"—she looked down at the name on the card— "Mr. Jeff Jackson."

Ménage was ready to conduct real business now. "Since you've never been here before," she said lustfully, "would you like to check out our VIP room, *Mr. Jackson?*"

Jeff gave Ménage a mischievous grin. He tucked his bottom lip in. He knew exactly what time it was. "I thought you'd never ask." He stood up and followed her all the way to the back of the club.

Denise pulled into the extravagant estate that belonged to no one other than Joseph Humphrey, a Platinum Crest Investment client that had been with her firm since the beginning. She had made Humphrey an incredible amount of money. He expressed his gratitude with gift cards to private spas and high-end department stores. He'd even given her a two-thousand-dollar Christmas gift one year. Tonight, Humphrey was celebrating his sixtieth birthday in style. But anything associated with Joseph Humphrey was sure to be a big deal, so Denise bent over backward to ensure that she maintained a piece of his portfolio. Even if it meant forging some of the documents to make the numbers match his expectations. She'd do anything to keep her clients happy, but lately, with the market's extreme downshift, that anything meant risky and creative accounting.

Wanting to look her absolute best, Denise wore a wine-colored evening gown with the platinum diamond necklace and tennis bracelet that Greg had bought her for Valentine's Day.

After handing the valet attendant her keys, she walked across the circular driveway and up the steps leading to the Humphrey's million-dollar home. She gave the door greeter her name and he checked it against the list. "Come right in, Mrs. Jackson," he said.

Piano music wafted through the Humphrey's entire home. Chandeliers and expensive furniture exhibited just how well off the family really was.

"Denise, you made it!" Claire Humphrey said, descending the swivel staircase. When she reached the bottom she walked over to Denise and smothered her in an overdone embrace. "You look marvelous, dear," she said.

"Thank you. And you're looking magnificently younger every day." Denise managed to conceal her true feelings about Claire. She had been the prime reason behind Joseph pulling out most of their money. Besides that, the woman had enough Botox in her face to last a lifetime. That reason alone made it difficult for Denise to look at her without wanting to laugh.

"Why, that's very kind of you," Claire said. "I try not to miss my facial appointments. It really makes a difference, you know."

"I'm sure."

"Let me find Joseph and inform him that you're here. He will be so pleased. In the meantime, make yourself at home."

"Thank you, Mrs. Humphrey. I'll do that." Denise began making her way through the room. She grabbed a glass of wine from one of the passing trays and perused the Humphrey's impeccable home. *One day*, she thought. *One day I'll be living just like this. With Greg.*

No sooner than she had that thought about Greg, a clear visual of him appeared only a few feet away. She blinked several times in disbelief. It was him. He was deeply involved in a conversation with Mr. Humphrey and another man who Denise didn't know. She quaffed the red wine before making her appearance known. She excused herself as she moved through the crowd of partygoers blocking her path. She moved swiftly across the room until she and Greg were only inches apart.

"Mr. Humphrey," Denise said, switching her eyes from Greg to Joseph.

"Denise, my dear. My wife and I didn't think you'd make it," he told her, reaching in for a warm hug.

"I wouldn't have missed it for the world, sir."

"Is Nadine here as well?" he questioned.

Denise was quick on her feet. "No, she's been ill. That's why she hasn't been in the office," she lied.

"Well, I'm sorry to hear that. And pardon my rudeness. Let me introduce you to my golfing buddies, Troy Perrigo, and Greg Adams, CEO of—"

"Adams Companies," Denise completed for him.

"I see you two have already met?"

"We're very well acquainted, yes," Denise answered, her smile transfixed on Greg.

Joseph brushed the corner of his nose and looked up at Troy. "Troy, I've been meaning to show you the new set of clubs Claire bought me for my birthday," he said.

"Oh, yes. Now's a better time than any," Troy said. "It was nice meeting you, Denise."

"The pleasure's all mine."

As the two of them vanished like thieves in the night, Denise lit into Greg. "Why haven't you returned any of my calls?"

Greg eyed Denise and then looked to the left side of the room.

After a moment, he settled his eyes on hers. "Business has been a little demanding lately. I'm sure you understand."

"Bullshit!" It took everything for Denise to contain herself and not make a scene.

"Will you keep your voice down?" he said through clenched teeth.

"I have called you numerous times. I've left message after message. Every time I've called, your secretary tells me you're not in... so don't stand here...and give me some nonsense bullshit about business being the reason."

"You asked for the reason and I just gave it to you. I haven't been available."

"I don't recall you letting business interfere whenever you were fucking my brains out at the office."

Greg's breathing became labored. "Look, we can talk about this tomorrow. I'll come by your place."

"Why tomorrow when I'm here now?" Denise asked, confused. As soon as she said it, a half-drunken white woman dressed in all black stumbled over to Greg.

"There you are, baby," the woman slurred. "I've been looking all over for you."

Denise looked at the woman. She was very attractive, slim, tanned, and appeared no older than Denise. Denise swallowed the lump in her throat and tried to calm the butterflies in her stomach. Who was this woman and where in the hell did she come from? She wanted to know. She looked in Greg's eyes, shaking her head, begging silently for him not to say what she believed he would.

"Denise," Greg started out. "I'd like for you to meet my wife, Vivian."

Denise nearly choked on her own spit.

Vivian outstretched her drunken hand. "Pleased to meet you, Denise."

Denise reluctantly accepted the woman's handshake, noticing the huge diamond that adorned her left ring finger in the process. "Likewise." Her eyes drifted to Greg's hand. Where a wedding band had never existed, it did now. Her head was spinning and she immediately felt the urge to vomit.

"Maybe we could discuss those figures in person tomorrow," Greg said. "I'll call you to confirm."

"But it's Sunday, honey," Vivian chimed in.

"Yeah. Tomorrow may not be a good idea. You should listen to your wife," Denise said sarcastically. She then turned to leave. Suddenly she wasn't in the partying spirit. She found her way back to the other side of the room and left the party just as quickly as she'd come.

21

Ménage took all of Jeff's ten inches inside of her warm, wet mouth. She sucked his dick with a greater purpose. He had money to blow and she wanted it all blown on her. As she bobbed up and down on his shaft, Jeff grabbed her by the hair and drove his dick deep inside her mouth. The numbing drops Ménage had taken earlier saved her the embarrassment of regurgitating all over him. Thankfully, she couldn't feel the pain of his massive meat stick playing hockey in the back of her throat.

"Oh fuck," Jeff hollered as Ménage bobbed faster than before.

Ménage let the length of his member slide out of her mouth, then instantly gripped it again and proceeded to suck him sideways.

Jeff was ready to explode. The entire time he had been fingering her hot pussy but now he was ready to introduce her to the real thing. He smacked her one good time on her ass and watched the way it bounced back like Jell-O. "Shit," he cursed under his breath.

Ménage grabbed a condom off the table and slid it on his hard-on. She turned in the opposite direction, straddled his lap and eased him inside of her. She did the trick off all tricks. She picked up her legs, folded them over his and fucked the shit out of him Indian-style.

"*Got damn*, baby!" Jeff hollered out.

Ménage wiggled her ass around in slow, circular motions. Jeff placed his hands around her tiny waist and bucked his pelvis like a mad bull until she began screaming in delight. He grunted loud but her screams were louder; good thing the music was louder than the both of them. Jeff's aggression gave her pause for a brief moment, but after that slight hesitation it began to feel so good she didn't care.

"Shit!" Jeff screamed as months of anguish poured out of him.

Monday morning he walked into the dealership feeling as if he'd found his manhood. "Good morning, ladies," he said, as he walked briskly past a group of women and headed straight for his office. He placed a cup of coffee on his desk and hung his jacket over the back of his chair. Seconds later Miss Janene was knocking at his door, although it was already open.

"Come in," he called out.

"Good morning, Mr. Jackson," Miss Janene said. "I just wanted to let you know that Calvin called out sick and Canvas called as well to say he's running a few minutes behind. His bus was late."

"Thanks for the update," Jeff said. He powered on his computer monitor and clicked on his email application. A moment later he looked up to find Miss Janene still standing in his doorway. "I'm sorry," he said. "Was there anything else?"

"No, sir," she lied. Truthfully she wondered why he looked so happy this morning. The past few mornings he'd come in looking like shit. "If you need me I'll be in the front."

"All right. Thanks again." Jeff got comfortable in his chair and began flipping through the three folders on his desk. He expected there to be much more. He pulled up a spreadsheet to check the company's inventory report, and to his surprise, they hadn't sold one single car in the past four weeks. He opened the three folders before him. They were all declines by the bank. He reviewed the credit reports and summaries as to why the loans had been declined. Bad credit, mostly. He sighed deeply and tried to figure out a way to turn things around. With the troubling economy people were afraid to take on any new debt and it was killing the car industry.

Jeff opened his internet browser so he could retrieve his emails. He had a ton of junk mail that he deleted all at once. While his concentration should have been solely on work, he couldn't stop thinking about Ménage and how badly he wanted to see her again. He had spent over four hundred dollars on her Saturday night, but it was the best four hundred dollars he'd ever spent. She made him forget about all of his problems. She made him feel like a man. For four hundred dollars she made him feel more alive than he'd felt since college.

"Mr. Jackson," Canvas blurted, inviting himself into Jeff's office.

"Good morning, Canvas," Jeff replied.

"Sir, Miss Janene said she didn't have anything for me to do so she asked me to check back here with you."

Jeff looked Canvas over. He was wearing one of the many suits Jeff had given him. "You look sharp today, man."

Canvas checked himself out. "I know this," he said, laughing cockily.

"Get your overconfident ass over here, man," Jeff said.

Canvas's big cheesy grin made Jeff wish for a second that he had a son. It was one of the reasons why he'd taken Canvas under his wing. Jeff never had a father around to show him how to dress and look professional the way he did now, so he took it upon himself to offer counsel to Canvas. He could relate to the young man.

He had told Canvas once before, "If you want people to take you seriously, you need to take yourself seriously." It was the code of ethics. Hell, for a black man, Jeff believed it was the law.

Jeff maximized the screen so that Canvas could read it. "You see these numbers here?" he asked.

"Yes, sir."

"Well, this number," he said, pointing to the zero, "isn't going to keep us in business."

Canvas nodded his head in agreement.

"How do you presume we change this?" Jeff sat back and waited for Canvas's response.

The young man's wheels were spinning. "I say we put on a show."

Jeff wasn't following. "A show?"

"Yeah, you know. Like a car show. I can round up some people I know who are in car cliques. We can get a big bouncy house for the kids, a face painter, a grill to get some barbeque going, and *shid*, it's on and poppin'."

Jeff sat back and let the idea marinate.

"I can even perform my single, 'Better Days,'" Canvas added.

Jeff was feeling the idea. "You know what; I think you're on to something."

"Think?"

"All right," Jeff said. "You are on to something. Let me just run it by corporate and make a few phone calls."

"So when are we doing this?"

"This weekend."

Canvas's eyes grew big.

"If you can't handle short deadlines, let me know," Jeff said, smiling.

"Naw, naw. I got it," Canvas answered, standing up from his seat. "Lemme get the ball rolling now."

"This is your chance," Jeff hollered to Canvas as the young man walked out the door.

Jeff's phone rang. He hit the intercom and Miss Janene's voice was clear in his ears. "Mr. Jackson, there's a Nadine Collins on line one for you."

Jeff thought about taking the call, but ultimately couldn't do it. He wasn't ready to deal with Nadine. Honestly, he wasn't sure if he ever would be. "Tell her I'm busy and I'll call her when I find the time."

"Okay, sir."

He disconnected the call, then pressed a different line to call Corporate.

22

"He's still not taking my calls," Nadine told her aunt. "He hates me."

"Honey. You have got to give him time to recuperate from all of this. Think about everything he's dealing with," her Aunt Mickey told her. "Have you thought about how he might be feeling? It was enough having Denise lie to him, but you, too?"

"I know but, I'm hurting."

"He's hurting!" Aunt Mickey said. "More than you'll ever know because men don't express themselves the way women do. That man's soul is broken, Nadine."

Nadine took a moment to collect herself. She had spent the entire two days she'd been in Atlanta pouring out her heart to her aunt. Mickey had become her sounding board and she was the only woman in the world that Nadine knew wouldn't judge her. Now as her aunt tried to get her to see Jeff's perspective, endless tears flooded Nadine's face. All she had done lately was cry, eat, and throw up. She was more miserable than she'd ever been in her entire life.

"You're making yourself sick, chile."

Nadine balled a Kleenex in her hand. "I know."

"Do you love him?"

Nadine only stared at her aunt. "Of course I love him."

"Do you believe he loves you?"

Nadine had to stop and think. "I don't know. I mean, I'm sure he does. Yes, he does. Why else would he cheat on his wife to be with me?"

Mickey looked at her niece incredulously. "Men cheat on their wives for various reasons. You said yourself that when the affair started he told you that he thought his wife was cheating. What makes you think his affair with you was actually about you? What if it was only retaliation against his wife?"

"Can't be."

"What makes you so sure, Nadine? If this man really loved you, do you think he would have hidden your relationship for three years?"

Nadine didn't want to answer that. "You're not making me feel better," she said weakly.

"Honey, I want you to wake up and smell the coffee. You're not the first woman going through something like this, and you won't be the last, either. But until you realize you're worth more than this, you'll keep settling." Mickey gently cupped Nadine's chin in her hand, lifted her niece's face so they could look at one another. Her smile was heartfelt and uplifting. "And I know I raised my baby better than that."

"You did," Nadine admitted. "But to be perfectly honest with you, Denise knew all along about Jeff and me."

"What?" Mickey said, floored by the new information.

"Yeah. Pretty pathetic, huh? Apparently we were her diversion so she wouldn't get caught doing her own dirt."

Mickey looked on in total disbelief. "I think I need a drink."

Denise walked around Platinum Crest Investments in a more pissed off mood than ever. She didn't even speak to Tonya and when her intern called out her name, she ignored him. She walked straight into her office and closed the door. She powered on her computer and began searching through the files in her desk for Greg's portfolio.

"That son of a bitch," she huffed. When she got her hand on his file, she pulled it out and began going through it. She located the address that he had listed on his paperwork. She began typing it in the search engine and just as she figured, one of his hotel properties pulled up. She took another deep breath and called the number he had listed as his home number. It reached one of his properties. There was one last number listed in his paperwork. She went into the White Pages online directory and did a reverse lookup. Same thing. Another number for one of his properties. She thought back to all of the times she had suggested they go to his place. Instead of taking her to his house, they would end up at some fancy hotel for the night.

For three years, Denise had been involved with a man who was living a double life. He had used her. He had lied. He had made a complete fool out of her and caused her to lose the best thing that ever happened to her. She snatched her phone off the hook to call him but Tonya came barging into her office before she could punch the first number.

"Mr. Adams is here to see you and he says it's urgent."

Denise placed the phone back on the receiver and got up from her chair. "Send him in," she said. She closed her office blinds and turned on her satellite radio to drown out the conversation they would have in the next few minutes. The second Greg walked his ass in her office and closed the door behind him, she slapped him.

Greg disregarded the stinging pain shooting through the entire left side of his face. "I deserved that," he said.

Denise's bottom lip trembled. "How could you?"

"I'm sorry," was all Greg could manage to say. He walked closer to her, apologizing profusely. "Baby, I'm sorry."

"Sorry won't do," Denise said. "I love you. I've given up so much for you."

Greg kissed her forehead as tears began to stream down her face. "I know," he said. "We'll get through this." Denise wrapped her arms around his neck. He slipped off his jacket and tossed it on the arm of the chair by her desk. He placed his lips on hers and kissed her passionately. His fingers moved through the roots of her hair as she moaned over and over. Her moans told him that, just that quickly, she had forgiven him and all was okay. His hands then found their way to her ass. He lifted her skirt, picked her up, and placed her on the edge of her desk.

Denise allowed Greg to have her the way that he had for the past three years. She was vulnerable and he knew it, but she wanted him more than anything in the world. They were just going through the motions. She propped her right leg up on a chair as his hands yanked off her panties and tossed them to the side. He then slid his dick inside of her. Denise didn't know what was happening as Greg took control of her body, her mind, and her soul. He was the devil in disguise. He had her doing things she never thought she'd do. "I can't do this," she uttered, coming to her senses. He pushed his dick further inside of her. "Stop. I can't, I can't do this."

"I'm almost there, baby," Greg said, stroking her so deep.

Denise opened her eyes. She pushed him away. "I'm not doing this!" she said, getting down from the desk.

Greg collected himself. He pulled his pants up and waited for his breathing to return to normal. "Do what?" he spat.

"I can't keep living a lie. I have a daughter to think about," she said finally.

Greg chuckled to himself. He wiped the sweat from his brow. "Whatever you say," he said.

"Tell your wife about me," Denise said. "Tell her that you're in love with another woman, and that you're leaving her."

Greg looked at Denise like she had lost her mind. "You can't be serious?" He frowned at her. "I mean, come on. Are you hearing yourself right now?"

Denise was shocked by his response. "So wait." She sighed. "I'm good enough to fuck but not to be committed to?"

"Denise, nobody told you to fall in love. You know the rules."

"Rules? What rules?"

Greg raised his hands. "Look, you're crazy if you think I'm telling my wife about you. I won't put her through that, so you can get that idea out of your pretty little head."

She looked at him with eyes that could kill. "You don't have to, because I will."

"You don't want to play hardball with me," Greg warned. "Trust me! My bite's much bigger than my bark."

"She has a right to know about me."

"Stay out of my marriage, Denise!"

"Or what?"

Greg narrowed his eyes until they were slits. He put on his jacket, and before he walked out of her office, left her with something to think about. He looked around the spacious room. "If you want to keep this nice little enterprise, then I suggest you stay in your lane." He smirked. "Have a beautiful day."

23

*J*eff felt lightheaded as he hung up from speaking with corporate headquarters. The news was unbelievable. "Why is this happening?" he said aloud. He placed a hand on his temple, further troubled by the start of a migraine. He checked his email for the second time and the confirmation of what he'd just been told was there in black and white. He printed off eight letters, his stomach rumbling with regret with each one. The worst part was the timing highlighted in each letter: effective immediately. Jeff had to push himself to continue but he sure as hell didn't want to.

He picked up the receiver and hit the intercom. "Ronald Lewis, report to my office. Extension 557, report to my office." Jeff straightened his posture, took a deep breath and readied himself for the worst possible thing he ever had to do in his entire career.

"What's up, boss?" Ronald asked, walking into Jeff's office. Ronald was the used car manager and had been with the company for over fourteen years.

"How you doing, man?" Jeff said in a meek tone.

"I'm good. What's up, though?"

"Ronald, since I've worked with you, I've known you to be a hardworking man. You've never called out sick, you've never complained, and you've always managed to pull your own weight."

Ronald gave his boss a perplexed look. "Thanks, man. But what you tryna tell me, boss?"

Jeff exhaled. This wasn't easy at all for him. He thought about the home Ronald had purchased with his wife three months prior. Thought of the excitement of the first-time homeowners. "Due to the economy, the company has decided to downsize in an effort to prevent bankruptcy," Jeff said in a monotone. "I'm sorry to inform you that, effective immediately, your position has been temporarily suspended until further notice." He handed Ronald one of the eight letters.

Ronald glanced at it. "Do you have any idea how long it's going to be before I'm rehired? I mean, come on, man, cut my hours, but don't cut my job," he pleaded.

"I won't know anything until Corporate notifies me. I'm sorry, man. It's not my call."

"I just bought a new house, man. My wife doesn't work. I have bills, insurance…man, give me a break. Unemployment ain't gonna save me here."

Jeff remained silent, but sympathized with Ronald. "If I hear something, you know you'll be the first person I call," he said.

"Damn." Ronald sighed. He got up from the chair and walked out of the office.

Jeff waited a few minutes before calling in the next five employees whose names were on the list. All were salesmen. One would have to get the news tomorrow when he returned to work because he was out sick today.

After Jeff got that group out of the way, he looked down at his last two letters. These would be the hardest for him. He picked up the phone, hit the intercom and said, "Janene Pierson, extension 546, please report to my office. Janene Pierson, extension 546."

Miss Janene walked in, sadness all over her face. "I already heard," she said.

Jeff handed her the letter, then stood up to give her a hug. "I'm so sorry, Miss Janene."

"It's okay. God wouldn't put me through this if He didn't think I would be all right," she said. She sniffled. "Since my husband took ill, I've been working my sixty-five-year-old butt off to take care of the both of us, ya know? It's about time I get a break." She smiled bravely.

"You take care of yourself," Jeff said. "And if you need anything, please don't hesitate to call."

Miss Janene nodded her head and headed toward the door. Canvas was walking in as she neared it.

"Mr. Jackson," Canvas said. "I made some phone calls and—Miss Janene, you okay?" She hurried past him, in tears. Canvas walked all the way into Jeff's office. "Is she all right?"

"I'm hoping," Jeff told him. He looked down at the last letter, which had Canvas's name on it.

"You sure? She seemed—"

"Go ahead with what you were going to say," Jeff cut in.

Canvas frowned, but continued. "Well, as I was saying, I called my crew and they down for the car show. I think we even got a plug to get it on the radio," he said excitedly. He noticed Jeff wasn't responding. "Mr. Jackson, you all right, man? You lookin' like you lost your best friend. What's going on around here today?"

"Canvas, I'm sorry to have to tell you this, but when I called Corporate this morning, I was informed that the company has decided to downsize." He spoke in the same monotone as earlier.

"And what exactly does that mean?" Canvas asked.

"It means that they have decided to eliminate or temporarily suspend positions until business picks back up."

Canvas waited for Jeff to hit him with the worst.

"They've sent me a list of employees that I have to let go. Effective immediately."

Canvas blew out his breath and shook his head. "And I suppose I made the list?"

"Yes. I'm sorry, man. I'll put a couple hundred dollars in your pocket to get you and your little sister through the month. And if y'all need to, y'all can come stay with me until you get on your feet."

"Naw, man. I got this." Canvas moved for the door. "I knew it wouldn't last. It was just a matter of time."

"Canvas, it's not the end of the world. Let me help you, man." Canvas headed out the door and didn't look back.

"Fuck!" Jeff yelled, knocking everything but his computer off his desk.

Nadine took another bite of the monkey bread her aunt had made and squealed in delight. It was so delicious. As she ate her second serving, she squinted her eyes at the small print on the computer screen. She decided to pick up the phone and dial the number for the Hope Cottage Adoption Agency in Dallas. After careful thought, she'd made up her mind to put the baby up for adoption.

"Hope Cottage, this is Carolyn, how may I direct your call?"

Nadine took a deep breath. "Hello, Carolyn," she began, "my name is Nadine Collins. I'm six months' pregnant and I would like to speak with someone about my options for adoption."

he scenery of the gentlemen's club was one Jeff had become all too familiar with. He was a regular customer now. Friday and Saturday nights. Dressed comfortably in a brown shirt and black jeans, he feasted his eyes on Ménage from a hidden corner of the main room. He drank three beers in thirty minutes and watched her grind her ass on another man's lap the same way she had done for him so many times before. Part of him felt a twinge of jealously. He turned his head, looked in the other direction, thought about getting into the groove of things. He had five hundred dollars in his pocket and tonight's plan was to treat himself to some extra fun. He was going to celebrate the finalization of his divorce in style. Denise had moved the process along rather quickly without them having to step one foot inside the courtroom. He let her keep everything; all he wanted for himself was peace of mind. So when the divorce decree arrived in the mail, he signed it without thinking twice. His marriage had been over more than three years ago; signing that paper just made it official.

"Want a dance?" an unfamiliar dancer asked, breaking Jeff's thoughts.

He looked beyond the woman and at Ménage. It was as if his favorite dancer hadn't noticed that he was even there. Not once did Ménage look in his direction. "Sure, why not," he said, turning his attention back to the new dancer. He reached for the almost empty bottle of beer, finished it off, and set his sights on the fine yellowbone straddling his lap. She had the name Black Ice tattooed on her left breast and double nipple rings in both her nipples. She worked the music into her hips while looking him dead in the eye and pushing his face in between her breasts. She did a number of dances on him until Ménage walked over and said, "I'll take care of him now." Black Ice smiled at Ménage, collected her payment, and left.

"Hey, baby," Ménage said, winking at Jeff.

"What's up?" Jeff replied, relaxed and hornier than ever.

"You're early. Why didn't you call me and let me know you were on your way? I would have waited on you," she purred as she slid her tongue in his earlobe.

"I wanted to surprise you," Jeff said, admiring how her ass had swallowed her purple g-string.

"I'll go freshen up and meet you back here in ten," she promised him.

Jeff bopped his head to the music. Suddenly it sounded better than ever. "Handle your business."

Ménage returned in ten minutes flat. That was all the time she needed to shower and reapply her makeup. She danced to three songs straight, a performance strictly for Jeff, before walking him back into the VIP room. Inside, she pushed him onto the leather couch and began unbuttoning his shirt. Kissed him nonstop as her hands traveled up and down his chest and into his pants. He unzipped the pants for easier access and, just as she expected, was hard as a rock. She stopped kissing him and redirected those kisses below. She kissed the mushroom tip, then slobbered all over it until it was nicely glazed. Jeff ran his hands through her hair, pulling slightly at her roots. Ménage gave him the best oral lap dance of his life.

"You think you can make tonight extra special for me?" he asked with a sly grin, hoping she could read his freaky mind.

Ménage licked his salty pre-cum off her lips and kissed him some more. She stopped briefly, walked out of the room and, within three minutes, returned with a full glass of ice. Jeff didn't know what Ménage had up her sleeve and he didn't give a damn. As long as it topped all the other nasty shit she had ever done for him. Things neither Denise or Nadine would ever be caught doing. Ménage took one of the cubes and gripped it between her lips. She placed the glass on the table and stood over Jeff. Before he could blink she was bent over backward in a half-handstand. Her legs were leveraged on his shoulders and her pussy stared him in the face. Soon Ménage's cool lips were wrapped around his member.

Jeff couldn't resist tasting her bubbly pearl. He pushed his face between her legs and inched his tongue along the edge of her arousal. His lips moved like a merry-go-round until he drove his tongue into her erotic core. He knew his actions were risky but tonight, he didn't care. He was a free man and free men could do whatever the hell they wanted to. Jeff felt as if, in any given moment, he would explode in her mouth. But before he did, the second half of Ménage's surprise entered in on the action.

Black Ice joined them in the VIP room. Ménage took one last tug at Jeff's dick and raised up. Jeff was so tipsy he barely recognized the woman who had danced for him earlier. Black Ice took one of the moon-shaped ice cubes from the glass and inserted it into her dry pussy while Ménage quickly slipped a condom over Jeff's stiffness. She squatted over him in a reverse cowgirl position and guided him inside of her. He filled her completely as soft moans escaped her lips. She used her vaginal muscles to control the ice dancing inside of her as she slid up and down his pole slowly before hitting overdrive.

Ménage eased down on Jeff's broad shoulders and lowered her pussy back into his mouth. He ate her sloppily, but she didn't care because the tag team show wasn't for her, it was for him. She and Black Ice were earning their wages by the nut, Jeff's nuts, and personal pleasure for them was of no significance. The faster Black Ice fucked Jeff, the faster and more insanely he ate Ménage. It was like a chain reaction. Just as Jeff felt himself letting go, Black Ice stopped riding him and escorted his dick into her mouth. She sucked him until he finally came down her throat.

"*Got damn*," Jeff grunted. He strained his eyes to see Ménage collecting payment from his wallet. Black Ice kissed him softly on the lips.

"Happy divorce, baby," Ménage said before heading off to her next customer.

Jeff sat in the secluded back room long enough to regain consciousness. He looked beside him, his wallet open and all of his cash gone. He chuckled at himself, wondering how it had gotten to this. Paying for sexual pleasures. "I'm losing my touch," he mumbled. He struggled to his feet, shaking off the mild headache flowering behind his eyes. He found his way to the door and back out front where pussy hungry men were packed together like wolves. He walked over to the bar and ordered a bottle of water.

"That'll be five dollars," the bartender said.

"You know what, never mind, man," Jeff said, walking off. He had been nickled-and-dimed enough tonight. On the way out of the club he looked for Ménage but didn't see her. When he looked up again, there she was giving some old man an exotic table dance. He shook his head and walked out of the club. While fishing for his keys in his pocket, he looked up and down the row of vehicles for his car. He deactivated the alarm from a distance and followed the chirping sound. He clumsily tripped over an empty bottle. He picked it up and tossed it in the grass. When he turned to open his car door he was staring down the barrel of a nickel-plated nine-millimeter.

"Nigga, give me all your money!" the masked man demanded.

Jeff looked at the faceless man. His first thought was to knock the wind out of the punk, but he decided against it when a voice from behind him said, "Don't even try it, playboy!" Jeff assumed two guns were drawn on him and disregarded his earlier thought.

"Look, my wallet's in my back pocket," Jeff said. "Take it and go before somebody gets hurt."

The robber behind Jeff reached into his back pocket. He pulled out the wallet and started searching through it for cash. He didn't find any, only credit cards.

"If it's money you're looking for, you're robbing the wrong cat. You might wanna catch me on the way *into* the club next time, not coming out."

The robber in front of Jeff hit him right over the head with the gun. "You think this a joke, motherfucker?" He cocked the pistol and forced it into Jeff's mouth.

Jeff breathed hard and balled his fists at his side. Something was telling him to show this lame-ass motherfucker that he wasn't a punk. He was half-drunk but his thoughts were as clear as the gun waving in his face.

"He ain't got shit, man, let's roll out."

Jeff felt the robber behind him sliding the wallet back into his back pocket.

The first gunman hesitated as he stared at Jeff through the mask.

"I said, let's roll, motherfucker. Before the cops get here!"

"Canvas, man, this mother—"

Jeff's body stiffened. He turned around. "Canvas? Don't tell me, man."

Canvas removed the ski mask.

"Man, what the fuck is you doing? You tryna get us busted, yo!"

"So this the road you decided to take?" Jeff asked, disappointed.

Canvas said nothing.

"Man, I'm ghost!" the other robber said, fleeing the scene.

"You don't have to do this, man," Jeff said.

"Man, this how I eat. This how I take care of mine!" Canvas hollered as if it was himself he was convincing.

"There are better ways. This right here, gonna get you locked up or killed!"

"Well, then I'm just gonna have to take that gamble," Canvas said, taking baby steps backward. "You have it all, so you wouldn't know what it's like out here in these streets! It's cold and niggas like me starvin', Mr. Jackson."

Jeff shook his head. "You're right! It's cold out here and niggas like you are starving. But you won't do your sister any good when you're lying up in a body bag. Because then the state becomes her mama, her daddy, and a substitute for her big brother."

25

"Thanks for agreeing to have lunch with me," Jeff told his ex-wife.

"I'm sure you didn't think I was going to pass up coming here?" Denise said playfully.

"I picked it for that reason," he said, and laughed. "I knew you couldn't resist."

Denise took a bite of her lemon and sucked the juice off her bottom lip. Followed that with a sip of water.

Jeff planned on saying everything that was on his mind to her today. About how the near-death episode at the club forced him to consider all the things he'd done. He thought about how differently it might've turned out that night, and how if it had, Denise would've never gotten to hear him say what he was about to say. She was the mother of his child. A child he had grown to love and call his own. Deandra had given him purpose. And, regardless of her deception, Denise was responsible for Deandra and the purpose Jeff had enjoyed for so many years. For that, he was beyond grateful. "I'm sorry," he told Denise.

Denise lowered her napkin and stared into her ex-husband's beautiful brown eyes. Her heart skipped a beat as the words traveled from his lips to her ears. She had hoped for this day and it had come sooner than she expected. Never mind that it should have been her who made the phone call to invite him to a wonderful lunch date. She had wanted to tell Jeff just how sorry and stupid she was for leaving him. That he'd done nothing wrong but love her. She wanted to beg him to take her back and forget everything bad that had happened between them. She wanted to start over and make things right. She wanted a second chance at love. At happiness. But as she looked in Jeff's eyes, deep within his soul, she knew that her time had run out.

"You don't have to apologize," she said.

"But I do."

"For what?"

"For hurting you. For lying to you." Jeff paused. "Denise, I'm sorry for not being enough."

Tears welled in Denise's eyes and she couldn't will them away no matter how hard she tried. Her aching soul cried out but Jeff had been bandaging his own wounds and healing his own heart. Denise had chosen to suffer in silence. God, she missed her husband. And the saddest part about it was that it took Greg treating her the way that he did for her to realize just how good of a man Jeff was.

Denise swallowed the emotion filling her throat. It was as bitter as the tears sliding down her unmade face. She briefly looked away, barely able to hold Jeff's gaze, but turned back because he deserved that much at least.

"Please say something," he said. "Anything."

"You don't have to apologize. I did this to us."

Jeff shook his head. "I take all the blame for this."

"I took you for granted when all you wanted to be was my husband," Denise said, crying. "I allowed another man...to destroy my marriage, while he kept his intact." Her lips trembled with every word.

"You don't have to do this," Jeff said.

Denise held up one finger, stopping him. "I forced you into

another woman's bed. My own best friend's," she said, shaking her head sideways. "I was selfish, naïve, and deceitful."

"Stop it! It was my mistake, and I take full ownership of it. I will not let you think, for one minute, that my affair was your fault," Jeff said. He exhaled. "I had been unhappy for quite some time. I should have been man enough to tell you instead of going behind your back."

"You didn't go behind my back," Denise said, hoping finally that he would see the true picture of how she had been the puppet master.

Jeff looked at her differently now.

"It started that night that I asked you to run errands for me at the church." Denise had his full attention now. "The two of you were making great conversation. Laughing. Getting along beautifully." She smiled, recalling every detail of that windy December night. "I had gotten there later than I anticipated, but I made it. I realized everyone had left but there were still two cars in the back parking lot."

Jeff shifted in his seat. His oily skin glistening with sweat as though it were fire coming out of her mouth, instead of this long overdue confession.

"I recognized both cars."

"Please don't do this," Jeff begged.

"I never said anything to either of you."

"Why did you let it go on? And why live with me, knowing that?"

Denise waited before she answered him. She now stared into thin air. "Because it was the perfect, twisted diversion."

"So for three years, you knew." Denise's silence confirmed his accusation. Jeff sat there in a world of his own. He had been seduced by lies all nine years of his marriage and where he thought he was cheating on his wife, he wasn't. It was a mutual affair.

"Do you hate me?" Denise asked. "For what I did to you?"

Jeff allowed the question to sink in before he answered. "No."

"Do you think I'm sick for allowing my husband to carry on an affair with my own best friend?"

"You had your reasons, Denise."

"You're making excuses for me."

The waiter walked over to their table with the bill. "Here you are, sir," he said.

Jeff smiled and pulled out his wallet. He placed a fifty on the tray. "Keep the change."

"You were saying?" Denise said.

"I don't think you're sick, crazy, psycho, or any of that shit." Jeff wiped his mouth with the black cloth napkin and tossed it back on the table. "You wanted out, and you found a way."

Denise went silent.

"No dead silence," Jeff ordered. "We passed that stage twenty minutes ago."

"I'm going to miss you," Denise said.

"Woman, you're acting like I'm dying." Jeff chuckled. "What do you mean you're gonna miss me? You've got the rest of your life to put up with me. Deandra will make sure of it."

"You got that right," she said.

"I'm full," Jeff said, rubbing his stomach. "I wouldn't mind catching a movie or something. Can you take off for the rest of the day, or do you have to report back?"

Denise rolled her neck. "Report back? Have you forgotten that I'm the boss?"

"Awww, that's right. I seem to be developing selective memory lately."

Denise stood up and grabbed him by the arm. "Come on, with your crazy ass. What am I going to do with you?"

Jeff took Denise by the hand and they walked out of the restaurant.

"By the way, how's the pregnancy coming along?"

Jeff looked down at his stomach and back at Denise. He placed the back of his hand over her forehead. "Okay, now I do think you're sick." He laughed.

Denise stopped walking and her hand fell out of his grasp. "Please don't tell me that she didn't tell you?"

The smile on Jeff's face disappeared. "Who? Tell me what, Denise?"

"Jeff," she said, "Nadine's pregnant. With *your* baby."

26

*D*enise received the call while she was in the movie theater. "I need to take this," she told Jeff, stepping out. It was the call she'd been waiting on all afternoon from the private investigator she'd hired only one day before. She walked to the front of the theatre. "This is Denise," she answered.

"Mrs. Jackson, I have that information you needed."

"Excellent." Denise reached in her purse and grabbed a pen. "Okay, I'm ready."

"His address is 68091 Shorecrest K in Frisco, Texas. It's a private address; that's why you haven't had any luck. It's not listed. I'll also email you a map because it won't pull up in the GPS."

"Are you there now?" Denise asked.

"I certainly am."

Denise checked the time on her cell phone. "I want you to stay there and guide me, in case I get lost. I'll check your email and then I'll be on my way."

Denise went back in the theater and watched the last few minutes of the movie. Thank goodness it was almost over. She and Jeff walked back to their cars and she told him what a wonderful time she had with him. But although Jeff and she went about their day as planned, Denise knew that what she had told him was bothering him. She knew Jeff and that was one thing about himself that he could never hide—his transparent expressions.

"Well, I'll catch up to you later," Denise said, giving him a kiss on the lips.

Jeff almost didn't respond and when he did, it was delayed. "Yeah, we'll have to do this again. Next time we'll bring Deandra."

"It's a date," Denise said, looking forward to it. She got in her car, reversed out of the parking lot, and got on the freeway. She called Iran back. "I'm in route," she said. He guided her the entire way.

The second Jeff reached Nadine's floor in her apartment building his heart dropped into the pit of his stomach. He'd thought about calling her but decided this was a conversation he'd rather have in person. He needed to be able to look her in the face.

He stopped at Nadine's door, stared at the doorbell, then finally pressed it. No sound came from her apartment or anywhere else. The entire building was utterly quiet. He pressed the bell again. Still no answer. He knocked. Nothing. Then it dawned on him. He still had a key. He reached in his pocket, pulled out the key, and let himself in. It was completely dark inside. He ran his hand down the left side of the wall until he found a light switch.

The apartment was unusually cold. He walked around Nadine's living room and nothing was out of place. He searched for anything that would confirm what Denise had told him earlier that day. He walked across the hardwood floor and into Nadine's bedroom. Nothing had changed. He checked his watch, wondering where she could be so late in the evening. He pulled out his cell phone and just as he was about to dial her number, the sound of someone's keys jangled on the other side of the door. He paced his breath. Listened hard. Heard a man's voice. Then he heard Nadine.

He hit the light switch and slipped behind the bedroom door. "What the fuck am I doing here like this?" he mumbled, beads of sweat forming on his forehead. Jeff knew this would look bad. Him being here, uninvited. He waited as the voices moved into the apartment. His heart pounding in fear of the unknown.

Nadine opened the door and flipped on the lights. "Thanks, Max," she told her neighbor as he set her luggage near the couch.

"You're more than welcome, Ms. Collins. You have a good night." Max turned to leave, shutting the door behind him.

Nadine removed her coat and laid it across her dining room chair. She rubbed her pregnant belly, then stopped mid-stroke. Her heightened senses filtered through to the memories of her baby's father. The smell of his cologne brought a weak smile to her face as she convinced herself that it was all in her head. She had left and gone to Atlanta to try and clear her head, but after stepping into her apartment, she realized that she hadn't cleared a damn thing. Jeff was just as much a part of her thoughts now as before she left.

She walked toward her bedroom, his scent tickling her nose with every step. She flipped on the light and when she looked up, Jeff was standing before her.

He stood in silence, his eyes drifting from her beautiful glowing face to her protruding belly.

"What are you doing here?" Nadine asked, surprisingly calm with the query. She hadn't jumped or screamed out. Her "Me against the world" attitude touched all parts of her new life. A thief or rapist would've been in trouble. Jeff even more so.

He stepped closer, his eyes studying her. "Is it mine?" he asked. Nadine didn't miss a beat. "Yes, he's yours."

"He?"

Nadine nodded her head, tears filling her unbelieving eyes. Superwoman reduced to tears that quickly. Emotional despite her best efforts to remain guarded, unaffected. "I tried to tell you sooner," she said.

Jeff placed a finger over her lips, silencing them. "Don't." He placed his hands on top of her stomach. "I'm here, Nadine."

Tears streamed from her eyes. She'd dreamed about a moment like this but it wasn't Jeff telling her he would be there for her that caused the tears. She had only come back to Dallas to meet with the family that she and the adoption agency selected for her unborn son. She'd completed all the preliminary paperwork, specifying her individual desires and characteristics of the adoptive couple, and had decided on an open adoption so that she could maintain communication with her child. The process thus far seemed rather simple, although it was the most difficult, yet unselfish decision she ever had to make. Nadine was also aware that she had the right to change her mind. The adoption was only binding and irrevocable once the legal papers were signed, which in her case would be immediately after delivery. But her mind was already made up. She was giving away the child she and Jeff had conceived out of love, out of lust, out of hurt. But how was she going to tell him that?

"I'm here for the both of you," Jeff said. "If you'll allow me." It seemed as though he were pleading with Nadine.

Nadine closed her eyes and opened them again. She knew there was no easy way to say what she was about to say, so she forced the words out of her mouth as fast as she could. "I'm not keeping him."

"What? What do you mean, you're not keeping him."

"I'm placing him up for adoption and..."

"Adoption!" Jeff stared at Nadine as though she were out of her mind. "Hell no. That ain't going down so you need to call whoever it is that you need to call and cancel that shit."

"Jeff, look at us!" Nadine said, her voice rising, echoing off the walls of her otherwise silent apartment. "I mean, come on. Give me a break."

"That's my son and I have every right to be a part of his life! We're keeping him."

Nadine exhaled deeply. She didn't know what to do. Jeff walked closer to her and cupped her chin.

"I'm right here," Jeff said. "We'll get through this together."

"I'm scared," Nadine admitted.

"I know." Jeff sighed. "But you have to trust me."

Nadine laid her head against his chest as he held her in his arms. Maybe this could work, she thought. "I'll inform the agency that I won't be going through with it."

Jeff was relieved that he could change her mind. He held her even tighter. "You're having my son," he said in almost a whisper.

Nadine nodded her head, silently hoping that she wasn't making the biggest mistake of her life.

Denise got out of her car and waved to Iran as he pulled off. Surprisingly so, the security guy bought her little white lie about checking in on her sick sister-in-law, Vivian. She even went as far as telling him that Greg had asked her for the favor since he would be getting home late, just for good measure. As she slowly made her way up the rounded cobblestone driveway, she marveled over the impeccable manicured lawn, palm trees, and lake that surrounded the Adams' million-dollar home. She was in total awe of the mansion's size, but expected nothing less. She looked around, hoping this would go exactly how she planned it. When she finally reached the front porch, she rang the doorbell.

There was complete silence.

Denise took a deep breath.

Vivian opened the door. "Hello," she said when she saw Denise.

Denise smiled at Vivian who was dressed from head to toe in a cabernet-red hip-hugging dress with black kitten heels. "Hello, Mrs. Adams, I'm Denise Jackson with Platinum Crest Investments. Remember we met—"

"At the Humphreys' dinner party," Vivian completed.

"Yes. Is Greg in?"

Vivian eyed Denise strangely.

"I only stopped by to go over some financials with him," she said, showing her the green folder with Greg's name on it.

"This late?" Vivian asked.

Denise gave her a warm smile. "Well, you know your husband is such a busy man. It was his request that I meet him here," she lied.

"Oh." Vivian gasped. "Well, come right in. I was just finishing dinner. You should join us," she said, allowing Denise inside.

"Don't mind if I do." Denise surveyed the immaculate home and its fancy décor. She could tell right off the bat that the woman was an art collector, judging by the fancy artwork hanging throughout. "Wow! You have a beautiful home, Mrs. Adams."

"Thank you. And please, just call me Vivian." She watched the way Denise's eyes roamed her home. "Come. Let me show you around."

Denise followed Vivian all through the house. She studied her, wondering what Greg saw in Vivian that he didn't see in her, besides the fact that she was white. Her racing thoughts forced her to remember how Greg had played her for a complete fool. She'd been too busy living in her own fantasy world to take the time to ask him something as simple as whether he was married, or involved with anyone, for that matter. Now she understood why he never offered to bring her to his place. She wasn't worth the risk. But now, Denise was fed up. She wasn't going to be the only one left out in the cold, hanging off a limb. She was dragging Greg's ass with her. She had lost and sacrificed so much. She was not going to let Greg walk away scot-fucking-free.

After the tour, Denise and Vivian walked back into the kitchen. Vivian poured two glasses of red wine. They made small talk as Vivian finished up dinner. To pass time they chatted about fashion, celebrities, and whatever came to mind. About a half a bottle in, they heard the door open and close to the garage.

"Honey, I'm home!" Greg announced, walking down the elongated hall. "Something smells good, baby!" He followed the smell.

When he turned the corner, his eyes nearly fell out of their sockets.

"Hard day's work, Mr. Adams?" Denise greeted. A sheepish smile played on her lips.

"What the fuck are you doing here?" he said through clenched teeth.

"Honey!" Vivian said, smiling as she came out of the kitchen. She walked over to Greg and gave him a kiss on the lips. "Dinner's almost ready."

Denise's own smile never left because the look on Greg's face was priceless. She grabbed the green folder off the counter. "I came to go over your financials. Did you forget you asked me to come?"

Greg raised his brow. He looked over at his wife, who was still smiling, and then at Denise. He cleared his throat. "I suppose I did," he said, following Denise's lead. "My schedule has been so hectic lately." He managed a half-hearted laugh. "I don't know if I'm coming or going half the time," he said slyly, feeling his armpits perspire.

"Well, you two go right ahead," Vivian said. "I'll finish up in here."

As soon as Vivian turned her back, Greg grabbed Denise by her elbow. He walked quickly down the hall and into his study, closing the double French doors behind them.

Denise yanked her arm back.

"What the hell do you think you're doing?" he lashed out at her.

Denise threw herself on him. She began kissing and groping him.

Greg grabbed her by both wrists and pinned her up against the wall. "Stop. This is over," he said sternly.

Denise shook her head. She'd hoped for one second that she could change his mind. Maybe she could save their relationship. Maybe she could convince Greg to leave his wife for her the way she had left Jeff for him. "Please," she begged. "I love you." Tears rolled out of her eyes.

"You're pathetic," Greg said, disgust washing all over his face.

"Leave her," Denise begged, allowing Greg to see just how weak she could be. He had claimed three years of her life and there was no way she was going to give up so easily. Not without a fight.

"I'm going to tell you one last time. You and I never happened!" he said. He pointed to her head. "It's all in there."

"So that's what you'll tell your wife?"

"You're damn right. I'll deny everything."

Denise shook her head. She felt desperate and used, all in one.

Greg backed away. "Now if you don't get the hell out of my house right now, I will make your days on earth a living hell."

Denise laughed at his last comment. She stared at him stone-

faced while mascara dripped down her face. "You already have."
She opened the door and walked out of the office. When she got
to the front of the house, she hollered out to Vivian. "Nice meeting you again."

"I hoped…you would stay…for dinner," Vivian said cautiously,
noticing how Denise's mascara was running down her face.

"Well, I just remembered that I have an important meeting in
the morning that I need to get prepared for," Denise said, forcing
a smile. "By the way, thanks for the wine."

"Anytime." Vivian smiled as well.

Greg escorted Denise out of his house and back toward her car.
Had he parked in the front as he normally did, he would have
seen her car and avoided her shenanigans.

Denise walked quickly, her mind finally made up. She got in
her car and slammed the door, cranking up the engine.

"I'll warn you not to pull this little stunt again!"

"Fuck you!" Denise screamed back. She was a woman scorned
and nothing mattered to her but getting even. "You have until
tomorrow morning."

"So you're threatening *me*?" Greg asked mockingly.

Denise put the car in reverse. "Tomorrow morning!" she said,
speeding off.

Greg walked back into the house, his wife standing there with
tears in her eyes. "So is that her?" she asked. "The woman that's
been keeping my husband company for the past three years."

Greg opened his mouth to lie. To say anything that would keep
his wife from knowing the truth.

"Don't!" Vivian raised her hand. "I heard everything. Besides,
I'm not a fool, Greg."

"Baby," Greg said, reaching for his wife.

Vivian was practically shaking. "Get out."

"What are you—"

"Get out!" Vivian screamed at the top of her lungs.

"No! I'm not leaving you like this."

Vivian grabbed the half-empty bottle of wine off the counter, ready to throw it at him. "I said, get the hell out!"

Greg looked at his wife, who was as distraught as she could be. "I'm sorry," he said.

Vivian cried even louder. "Just go."

Greg grabbed his keys from the counter and left.

27

*S*till half-asleep, Denise walked through Platinum Crest Investments looking as if she'd just crawled out of bed and driven straight to work. Her hair was pulled back in a loose ponytail and she didn't have an ounce of makeup on.

"Mrs. Jackson," Tonya said in a panic. "The auditors are here."

Denise's eyes opened wide. "Auditors! Why are we being audited again?"

Tonya shook her head profusely. "I have no idea."

Denise stormed to the back and found two suitably dressed individuals, a man and a woman, in her office. "May I help you?" she asked.

"Hi, I'm Sharon Crowell," the woman said, extending her hand to Denise.

Denise looked at it. "I was audited four months ago. There must be some mistake."

Sharon looked over at her partner. "Bill and I would like to start with all of Platinum Crest's portfolios."

Denise walked around the woman and over to her desk. She snatched up her phone from the receiver. "Jim, will you please come show our visitors to the file room?"

"Yes, ma'am, Mrs. Jackson, I'll be right there."

Denise looked at the auditors suspiciously. "May I offer you anything to drink?" she asked.

"No thank you," they said in unison.

Jim appeared in Denise's doorway. "Good morning," he spoke to everyone.

"Jim will show you to our file room," Denise said kindly.

Jim led them out of Denise's office and down the hall. Denise flopped down in her chair. "This is the last damn thing I need," she said, and grunted.

"Is there anything I can do?" Tonya asked.

"No." Denise smiled up at her. "Just hold all my calls, please."

"Sure thing."

Denise powered on her computer and attempted to go about her day as usual. She thought about last night and how Greg had practically shoved her out of his life. She loved him and hated to do what he was forcing her to do, but it was only right that Vivian know about her husband's three-year-long affair. Denise glanced over at the clock. It was a few minutes past nine. She thought about calling Greg, hoping that maybe he had come to his senses. Those thoughts of Greg quickly faded, though, when her cell phone lit up. It was a number she didn't recognize but she answered anyway.

"This is Denise."

"Mrs. Jackson, this is Nurse Stella at Madison Elementary. I have your daughter here and she said she's not feeling well. I think it may be a stomach ache. She doesn't have a fever."

Denise pulled the phone closer to her ear. "May I speak with her, please?"

"Sure."

Seconds later Deandra was on the phone. "Mama?" Deandra said.

"Hey, baby. Are you okay?"

"No. My tummy hurts really bad," Deandra said.

Denise looked out her window and saw that the clouds had gotten much darker. "I'll tell you what. Would you like for me to call Grandma and have her come get you?"

"Yes," Deandra said softly.

"Okay, well, I'll call her now. But too bad we'll have to miss out on ice cream sundaes tonight," she said.

"No. I should feel better by then, Mama."

Denise chuckled lightly. "All right. Well, Mama will see you tonight."

"Okay."

"Deandra," Denise said before her daughter hung up.

"Yes, Mama?"

"I love you."

"I love you, too, Mama," Deandra said before handing the phone back to her nurse.

"Mrs. Jackson, will you be picking her up?" Nurse Stella asked.

"No, I'm going to send my mother, Grace Henry. She should be on the pickup records."

"Okay. Just let her know Deandra will be here at the clinic."

"Thank you," Denise said before hanging up and calling her mom. Her mother answered in her normal energetic voice. "Hello, Mama," Denise said.

"Hey, Suga Pea," Grace replied.

"Will you do me a favor?"

"I should have known," Grace said, laughing.

"Hey, that hurt!" Denise laughed.

"You know I'm only kidding. What can your ole mama do for you, baby?"

"It's Deandra. She's sick."

"Oh. Is she running a fever?"

"No. Just an upset stomach."

"I think I might have something here for that."

"Good. Will you pick her up for me, please? It's just that I have these auditors here and I don't want to leave."

"Don't you worry. I'm grabbing my purse now."

"Okay. Well, you be careful out there because it looks like we're about to have a storm."

"Yeah, the weather man said it's going to get ugly. Well, let me skip on out so we don't get caught in it."

"Okay, Mama. And if I never told you, I want you to know that I really appreciate everything you do for me."

"That's what mothers are for, Denise. I love you, suga."

"I love you, too, Mama."

Denise ended the call just as Tonya walked in her office. "I have someone trying to reach Nadine. What do I tell them?"

Denise looked at the stack of papers piled on her desk. Underneath them was the resignation notice Nadine had given her. Denise had yet to look at the letter or file an amendment to have Nadine removed as partner. So, technically, Nadine still owned fifty percent of Platinum Crest Investments.

"Tell them she's on vacation," Denise said.

Tonya looked at her strangely. "Ooookay. I'll do that."

Denise returned to her work. Two hours later she received a phone call from the man who had turned her world completely upside down. "What do you want with me, Greg?" Denise lashed out. He had insisted that Tonya put him through. Telling her it was of extreme importance.

"My, aren't we a bit feisty today?"

"I have a lot of work to do."

"I'm sure you do. Especially with those auditors breathing down your neck."

"I'm not in the mood—" Denise stopped midsentence. "How

did you know that I had auditors here?" Greg was silent but she could hear him breathing through the phone. "How did you know that I had auditors here?" she repeated.

"I told you not to fuck with me. You made the biggest mistake of your life showing up at my house last night!"

"You son of a bitch!" Denise sprang up from her chair, slammed the phone down and walked quickly down the hall. She walked into the file room and confronted the auditors, the both of them busy going through her clients' records. The violation felt like a raw wound. "Did Greg Adams send you here?" Denise shouted.

The auditors looked at each other quizzically. "I'm not sure we know what you mean," Bill said.

"You know exactly what I mean," Denise barked. "Greg Adams. Did...he...send you?"

"Mrs. Jackson, we're with the Securities and Exchange Commission. We've never heard of a Greg Adams." They pulled out their credentials and handed them forward for her to examine.

They looked legitimate.

Denise was losing her mind. She walked up the hall to find Tonya at her desk. "Did you tell anyone that we were being audited?"

Tonya shook her head, eyeing her boss with a concerned look on her face. "Wait," she said. "I may have mentioned it when Mr. Adams called. That's only because he insisted on speaking with you. I told him you were busy with—"

Denise exhaled. "It's okay." She touched her chest, felt her heart racing, fought to settle her breathing. "I need to go take care of something. I'll be back," she told Tonya. Then she walked back into her office, grabbed her purse, and left.

She drove at racing speeds in the pouring rain on the freeway, ready to give Greg a piece of her mind, face to face. She hated that she ever met him. She raised the volume on the radio. A woman was singing her heart out about being in love and being hurt. Denise changed the station. She was sick of love. Sick of pain. Her cell phone rang in her purse but she ignored it. She was too upset to speak to anyone. She switched from lane to lane, swerving in and out of traffic. The ringing started up again. She snatched the phone from her purse and, without looking at the caller-ID display, she answered.

"This is Denise."

"So what's going on in that pretty little head of yours now, huh?" Greg asked.

"You son of a bitch! This isn't over, you understand me? I'm on my way to speak with your wife right now," she lied.

"You're too late, Denise! I told her everything last night."

"You're lying!"

"No, I'm not. Now I've told you to stop all this madness and go on with your life in peace."

"Three years, Greg!" Tears poured down Denise's face. "I gave you three fucking years!"

"And your point is?"

Denise was furious and the hot tears that fell from her red puffy eyes made everything before her a blur.

"Now, if you know what's best for you, you'll turn around, and go back to work."

"Go to Hell!" Denise screamed, tossing her phone back into her purse. In the blink of an eye, the car before her slammed on its brakes, causing Denise to slam on hers, too. Unable to stop completely, she quickly switched to the left lane to avoid hitting the other car, but neglected to notice the eighty-thousand-pound semi-truck traveling sixty-five miles per hour.

The trucker braked as fast as he could but the weight of his truck sent him sliding into the back of Denise's car.

28

"Good morning, sleepyhead," Nadine said, walking into her bedroom. She placed a folding tray over Jeff's lap and gave him a kiss. It was raining hard outside. Although Nadine hated when it rained, it was the perfect weather for what she had in mind.

"Damn," Jeff said. "All this? I might need to take a vacation more often, if this is the type of treatment I get." He stared down at the Belgian waffles, sausages, hash browns, and scrambled eggs on his tray as Nadine poured fresh orange juice into a glass. He sat up completely. "Are y'all going to join me?"

Nadine rubbed her belly. "Canvas and I ate earlier this morning," she said, and smiled. She was so glad that Jeff had agreed to the name for their baby. And the biggest coincidence was when he told her that he had that exact name in mind. She was so happy now that Jeff was back in her life and she couldn't wait for them to be one big happy family. She dreamt of it every night and her wish was slowly coming true. They talked for hours the night before about the pregnancy and how she was progressing. She showed him the sonogram pictures and the DVDs for the first time. He apologized for not being there for her sooner. She told him the sole reason she originally wanted to put the child up for adoption, thinking it would be the best thing for the baby. But today was a new day, and as she watched Jeff eat, she told herself that this was how it should have been. They were meant to be in each other's lives and the baby growing inside of her stomach was confirmation of that.

After Jeff was completely finished eating, Nadine took the dishes to the kitchen and cleaned them, put them away and joined Jeff in bed. She lay in his arms and spoke of the happiness she now felt. They kissed until Jeff began easing off her nightgown. It had been months since they made love but he would never forget the way it felt being inside of her. He kissed his way down her neck, her breasts, her stomach, and then opened up her thick thighs and kissed her there. She grabbed him by his head and wrapped her legs completely around his back. Jeff parted the lips of her pussy with his fingers and licked up and down. He then took the tip of her clit between his lips and sucked on it gently.

"Oh, baby," Nadine moaned. She felt her pussy getting wetter and wetter as his lips massaged her. She closed her eyes and rocked with his face. Soon his long thick tongue was pressing through her creamy folds. "Oh shit, Jeff." She cursed and called out his name. The rain beat against the windows and, for once, Nadine welcomed the sound. Jeff increased his speed and his tongue began backstroking out of her river and back around her clit. It did its own little tap-dance that drove Nadine insane.

"Cum for daddy," Jeff sang, telling *his* pussy exactly what he wanted it to do.

Those words were like music to Nadine's ears. She did exactly what he asked. She came for him so hard that she thought her water broke.

Jeff got up, laid on his back, and Nadine straddled him. She eased him between her legs and let out a sensual moan as his dick stood straight up inside of her. She rode him slow, but her pussy was squeezing him so tight that the slightest sway in her hips nearly had him erupting. He cupped her swollen breasts in the palms of his hands, leaving only her hardened nipples uncovered.

"I love you so much," Nadine said as she rode him.

"I love you too, baby," Jeff replied, concentrating more on dropping his load inside of her. Nadine threw her pussy on him so good he was sweating.

"Will you marry me?" she asked Jeff whose eyes were seemingly rolling in the back of his head.

"Yes!"

"You will?"

"Yes, baby. I'll marry you," he said, just before unleashing an explosive orgasm.

Thirty minutes later and Jeff was still lying in the exact same spot. He was flipping through the television channels as Nadine lay beside him, sound asleep. He thought about Nadine's marriage proposal and his own acceptance, asked himself now if it was the best thing to do. There were no doubts in his mind that the baby she was carrying was his. He was also positively certain that Nadine loved him. But the question that still played in his head was whether he was truly ready to walk down the aisle again. He thought about Deandra and the effect it would have on her once she realized her godmother was marrying her daddy.

The answers didn't come fast enough, making Jeff all the more desperate. Unable to find anything on TV to hold his interest, he parked it on the news.

"Well, what you're looking at right now behind me is the nasty aftermath of what happened a short moment ago when this eighty-thousand-pound semi-truck jack-knifed in the middle of Interstate 30, sending

one car colliding into the median, and causing a four-car pileup. As you can see traffic is at a standstill and tow trucks are having a hard time forcing their way to the scene. It seems that the rain may have been a contributing factor but we still do not have all of the details as to what took place here this morning." The reporter paused and placed her hand over her earpiece then brought the microphone back up to her mouth. "*It's now being reported that two people are in serious condition and are now being airlifted by a CareFlite helicopter to Parkland Memorial Hospital.*" The reporter turned to the witness standing beside her. A Hispanic man. "*Sir, could you please tell us what you saw?*"

"*The black Chrysler was going pretty fast to begin with. Then it jumped in that guy's lane and he rammed in the back of it. I had my kids in the backseat so I pulled over to the far right and just waited. It all happened so fast.*"

"*Thank you, sir.*" The reporter pointed to the car that was completely smashed in on the driver's side. "*This is the vehicle our witness just finished describing and, as you can see, it's hardly recognizable.*"

Jeff cringed at the sight of the car. "It'll be a miracle if they make it out of that alive," he said under his breath.

He lowered the volume on the television, got out of bed, and walked into the bathroom. He turned on the shower while he looked for something to wear but the chirping sound coming from his cell phone sent him in the other direction. He walked as quietly as he could through the living room, completely naked, and grabbed his phone off the counter. Saw that he had six text messages. All from Ménage. He read every one of them and couldn't deny how tempting it was to make the trip to see her. He started to reply, to tell her that he missed her, too. That he was just as horny. And that he'd take her up on her offer of another round on the house. He grabbed at his dick. That quickly it had gotten hard. Another message came through. This time there was an attachment.

Jeff downloaded the picture of Ménage and all kind of freaky shit flooded his corrupted mind. She was lying in bed completely naked. Her legs were wide open and her shaved pussy was covered in whip cream with a cherry buried in it. Another message came through.

Don't you want to come pop my cherry?

Jeff looked around to check if Nadine was still sleeping. She was. He immediately replied: *Hell yes! When?*

Now!

Jeff licked the anticipation from his lips. He weighed his options. Hell, he wasn't married yet and he and Nadine were just getting back to the point of speaking. He didn't see any harm in getting Ménage out of his system, once and for all. He replied right back.

I'm walking out the door now.

Here's my address. 75120 Keligore Pkwy. Apt 237.

Jeff flipped his phone closed, showered and then dressed. He wrote a quick note for Nadine and placed it on the nightstand beside her bed. Said he was going to check on his apartment and grab some more clothes. He wasn't lying, he just wasn't telling the whole truth. He locked the door behind him and made his way to his car. When he got in, he punched Ménage's address into the navigational system and prepared himself for whatever she had in store.

Adina Howard's "Nasty Grind" flowed through the speakers hanging from Ménage's champagne-colored walls. She answered the door in her silver seven-inch slingback stilettos. Only silver pasties covered her perfectly round chocolate nipples. Jeff's knees nearly buckled when his eyes made it to the sheer white thong she wore. Ménage laughed and kissed him on the lips and guided him by the hand inside of her small apartment. He closed and locked the door behind him, followed her down the walkway and into her candlelit bedroom. A sweet vanilla scent danced over his nose as he slipped off his jacket and laid it on a nearby chair. He checked out all the toys she had laid out on the nightstand beside her bed. There were pink fur handcuffs, a feather, anal beads, lubricant, and three condoms.

"I see you were serious about missing me," Jeff said.

"As serious as a heart attack," Menage admitted, kissing him until their tongues intertwined. She forced Jeff onto the bed and climbed on top of him, kissing him some more. She swept her long hair weave to the left side of her neck and began lifting up Jeff's shirt. Her tongue traced his six-pack and around his navel. She unbuttoned his jeans, slid off his pants and boxers, and began waking up his dick with her warm mouth. She sucked Jeff's shaft from the top to the bottom until the heartbeat of his veins was pumping in her mouth.

Jeff loved the feeling of being sexed like this and Adina was right, Ménage was a freak, just like him. He wanted to dip into her candy bowl but she was too busy tea-bagging him. He refused to interrupt. His cell phone started ringing and he thought about answering it before things got even more heated. Ménage cancelled the thought, grabbing his pants off the floor and fishing through the pockets for his phone. Once she found it, she powered it off without a second thought.

"You're on my time now, daddy," she said, easing his dick back in her mouth.

Jeff lay back, completely relaxed, and let Ménage have her way.

Besides, the pussy was on the house, so there was no way in hell he was passing an offer this sweet up.

Three hours later Jeff showed up to Nadine's again. He unlocked the door to find her completely dressed and in tears. "Baby, what's wrong!" he said, rushing toward her in a panic.

Nadine could barely get it out. "It's...it's..." She started to cough and Jeff ran to the bathroom looking for her inhaler. Once he realized it wasn't there, he rushed to find her purse.

"Here, baby! Calm down."

Nadine squeezed a few puffs into her mouth, unending tears streaming down her face. Jeff rubbed her shoulders as her breathing slowly returned to normal and her coughing ceased.

"Where have you been?" Nadine yelled. "We've been calling you and calling you but you never picked up."

"Is the baby okay?" Jeff asked, worry all over his face.

Nadine nodded. "It's not the baby. It's Denise."

Jeff's heart began to pound. "What about Denise?"

Nadine's bloodshot eyes were steady on Jeff's. "She's been in a horrible car accident," she said, and sniffed, "and they don't know if she's going to make it."

29

*J*eff and Nadine rushed through the doors of Parkland Hospital's emergency room. Jeff attempted to calm Nadine the entire drive, afraid that she would suffer another asthma attack. But his efforts were thwarted by his own worry. He'd called Grace for details and what she'd told him made him think the worst.

Once inside, Jeff walked straight over to the information booth. "I'm looking for Denise Jackson," he rattled off. "She was brought in this morning."

Nadine waited patiently behind Jeff, her eyes still burning with tears and roaming around the crowded county hospital. The three-part sequestered waiting area was overflowing with sick or injured people waiting to hear their names called.

"She's in the intensive care unit," the desk clerk said to Jeff, handing him a slip of paper with the information on it.

"Thanks." Jeff took the paper and led Nadine by the hand to the other side of the hospital.

"Daddy!" Deandra yelled once Jeff hit the corner of the waiting area.

Jeff let Nadine's hand fall from his before Deandra could notice. "Hey, baby," he said, bending over to hug her tightly. He framed her face with his hands. "Are you all right?"

Deandra's tear-filled eyes said it all but she nodded her head anyway.

"Where's Grandma?"

"She went to the restroom," Deandra said.

"And where's my hug, little girl?" Nadine asked, stretching her arms out to Deandra.

"Hey," Deandra said dryly. She looked at Nadine's round belly. "Are you having a baby?" she asked.

Nadine looked at Jeff, then inhaled deeply before answering her goddaughter. "Yes, I'm having a little boy."

Deandra turned her head and rolled her eyes.

"You made it!" Grace said, walking up from behind them. She gave Jeff a hug. Then said, "Hello, Nadine," while eyeing her daughter's ex-best friend peculiarly.

"Hi, Miss Grace."

Grace's gaze dropped to Nadine's stomach. She inhaled, then closed her eyes, shaking her head. She grabbed Deandra by the hand. "The nurse said we can go back two at a time to see her."

Jeff nodded. "Okay. We'll be right here."

Grace and Deandra walked out of the waiting area and through the double doors of the intensive care unit. They found Denise's nurse and she led them to Denise's room.

Once Grace laid her eyes on her daughter's motionless body she nearly hit the floor. Her legs weakened as she struggled to keep standing.

Deandra started crying at the sight of her mom with tubes stuffed down her throat.

Grace managed to make it to the bed. "My baby," she cried, tracing her shaky fingers over Denise's face.

Deandra placed her hand into her mom's. "Mommy, please don't leave me," she begged, as more tears flooded her face. "Mommy, Mommy, Mommy." She kept saying it, hopeful her words would make her mother wake up.

"We're right here, baby," Grace said weakly. "You're a fighter so I know you'll get through this." Grace had all her prayer warriors on top of it. She'd even called her pastor and his wife who were already on their way to the hospital.

As the computer monitors chirped loudly and the confined room turned cold, Grace took Deandra by the hand. She placed her other hand on top of her daughter's forehead and began reciting "The Lord's Prayer."

Our Father, who art in heaven, hallowed be Thy name. Thy Kingdom come, Thy will be done, on earth as it is in heaven. Give us this day our daily bread. And forgive us our trespasses, as we forgive those who trespass against us. And lead us not into temptation, but deliver us from evil. For Thine is the kingdom, the power and the glory, for ever and ever. Amen.

Jeff waited and waited. He and Nadine were both unnerved by the families around them. There was so much going through Jeff's head but he didn't want to focus on his thoughts. He just wanted Denise to come out of this alive.

"I'm going to go use the restroom," Nadine said, getting up.

"All right," Jeff said, leaning his head back against the wall.

"Mr. Jackson!" Tonya said, rushing up to him. "We came as soon as I got the call."

Jeff recognized the receptionist for Platinum Crest right away. He stood and gave her a hug. "Thanks for coming," he said.

Tonya introduced her husband. "Mr. Jackson, this is Lee."

"Glad to meet you, my man," Jeff said, shaking his hand.

Lee and Tonya took a seat beside Jeff. "So have they said anything else?"

"No. We're just praying for her to pull through."

"And she will," Tonya said, sounding so assured. She placed her purse on the side of her. "We just have to believe that." She recalled how stressed Denise had been acting lately, especially earlier that morning.

"Hey, you two," Nadine said, returning from her bathroom break. She gave Tonya and Lee a hug.

"Hey, honey. I haven't seen you in months," Tonya said. "You don't come around anymore."

"I've been out of town," Nadine said. "I went to visit my aunt."

"Oh. Vacation."

"Yeah."

"Well, that's good. You're looking good." She glanced down at Nadine's belly.

"Thank you." Nadine smiled softly, taking her seat on the other side of Jeff.

Tonya tried to make small talk to get everyone's mind off of the reason they were all gathered there. "Well, Lee and I might have one in the oven finally," Tonya told Nadine.

"That's great," Nadine replied, happy for them.

Now Jeff wished they would change the subject.

"I want a girl so bad," Tonya said. "Have you found out what you're having?"

Nadine cleared her throat before she answered. "It's a boy."

Tonya smiled. "My, my, my. You're going to have your hands full."

Nadine nodded in agreement.

"Well, when's the shower?"

"I'm not having one," Nadine said.

Tonya gave her a look. "Why? I mean, it is your first baby," she said.

Nadine looked at Jeff. He was quiet and in a world of his own. Nadine shrugged her shoulders. "I don't know. It was a last-minute decision."

Grace and Deandra came walking back into the waiting area. Jeff and the others all stood to their feet. "How is she doing?" Jeff asked, anxious.

Grace could barely get her words out. She shook her head. "She's not responding. My baby's just laying there." She cried and took a moment to gather herself. "She looks like she's sleeping."

Deandra's tears started to flow. She sobbed so strongly her entire body shook.

Nadine walked over to console her. "Come to Auntie Na—"

"Don't touch me!" Deandra lashed out at her. "I hate you! You stole Daddy away from Mommy and me." Her accusation grabbed everyone's attention.

Nadine stood frozen in place. Tonya, Lee, and every other person in the waiting room stared at her. Tears began streaming down her face.

Jeff reached out to Deandra but she rejected him and stood behind her grandmother.

"I'll talk to her," Grace told Jeff.

Tonya shook her head. "So, wait, are you telling me that's Denise's husband's baby?" she asked for clarification.

Nadine didn't say a word.

Jeff intervened. "It's nobody's damn business!" he said loud enough for everyone in earshot to hear.

Lee pulled Tonya by the hand but she didn't budge. "You should be ashamed of yourself," she told Nadine.

"Look, you don't know the half of it, so please don't judge me," Nadine said sternly, completely humiliated by everything unfolding.

"Know the half of it?" Tonya pursed her lips. "You're pregnant by your best friend's husband. I can see the other half of it."

"Could you watch your mouth? My daughter's right here," Jeff said.

"Man, don't raise your voice at my wife like that," Lee said.

"It's trifling homewreckers like you that make it hard for women like me!"

"I'm not going to stand here and take this," Nadine said, grabbing her purse off the chair. "Denise was my best friend and I loved her like a sister! If any of you knew the truth, you'd feel differently." She shook her head and pressed her lips together tightly.

"Calm down," Jeff said, standing in between the women.

"What are you saying, Nadine? That my daughter caused all of this?" Grace asked, motioning at Nadine's stomach.

Nadine looked at Grace and shook her head. "I'm saying Denise wasn't innocent." Her breaths were labored as she turned to walk out of the rowdy room. She moved down the hall and through the double doors of the ICU and into Denise's room.

Nadine immediately noticed all of the machines Denise was hooked up to as she lay helpless in a medically-induced coma. Several thick bandages covered Denise's head as well as the scars and cuts on her arms. Nadine suspected major head trauma, a slim chance of full recovery.

She walked closer to the bed and placed her hands on top of Denise's body. "I hope you can hear me," she began, sniffling. "I know a lot has happened between us these past few months... and...a lot of things have gone unsaid." Nadine stopped in the middle of her sentence. "But I want you to know that I'm sorry." Sniff. "You were and still are my only friend, Denise. I could tell you anything." Nadine dropped her head and then raised it again. She placed her hand into Denise's and gave it a soft squeeze. "I love you." Those were her last words to her friend before the monitors started going crazy.

"*Code Blue!*" a nurse yelled as a group of them rushed into the room and over to Denise.

"We need you to step out, please!"

"Why?" Nadine protested. "What's happening to her?"

"Ma'am, we need you to step out!" one of the nurses ordered Nadine.

"Please, God, don't take my friend!" Nadine screamed. "Denise. Oh, God…oh, God!"

She continued to yell as one of the male nurses dragged her out of the room.

30

*T*he parking lot of the church was completely filled with cars. Some funeral attendees were making their way inside the building as the shiny black stretch limo pulled alongside the front. The limo driver stepped out and walked to the rear of the car where Deandra and her grandmother were. He took Grace and Deandra by the hand, and escorted them into the building.

Everyone that entered the service was handed an obituary program. When the family began walking inside, everyone rose to their feet.

Grace, who was dressed in solid black with a bright yellow flower resting over her heart, could not believe that she was sending her only child home. Her baby. With her head slightly bowed as they moved indoors, Grace concentrated on the low music playing. She waved her gloved hand in the air as she was escorted to the front pew.

Grace and Deandra took their seats. For the first time Grace looked up and saw the pearl-and-gold-trimmed casket that her daughter's body lay in. Shudders moved through her with a deeper force as she struggled to look at it. Her grandbaby also began crying at the sight.

Deandra's cries triggered all the others that followed. "Mommy!" she cried. Jeff and Nadine had been in one of the three Town Cars following the limo. The two of them walked in, dressed in solid black, sadness covering their faces.

Jeff took one look at the casket and nearly buckled over. A tight feeling settled in the pit of his stomach and moved through his lungs. He couldn't breathe, and before he knew it, tears showered his face as his daughter's cries rang in his ears.

He and Nadine joined Grace and Deandra on the first row. Directly behind them was extended family, both his and Denise's co-workers, along with a host of Denise's clients. Tonya, seated directly behind Jeff, kept her head lowered in sadness.

Nadine hadn't slept well for three days because of the stress and loss of Denise. She'd cried every night. And just today she'd started experiencing light vaginal bleeding, too. Could life get any worse? She lowered her head and allowed tears to fall in her lap.

Once the doors of the church closed, the choir director stood up and motioned for the choir to stand to their feet as well. He guided them with his hands and they immediately started the celebration of Denise's homegoing in the fashion their dear friend and old choir member would have wanted.

Soon and very soon, we are going to see the King. Soon and very soon, we are going to see the King. Hallelujah, Hallelujah, we are going to see the King. No more cryin' there…we are going to see the King… Hallelujah, Hallelujah we are going to see the King. No more cryin' there… we are going to see the King…

Cries erupted throughout the sanctuary as the choir chanted the lyrics of the song. Sorrow swept through everyone as the knowledge of Denise's untimely death sank in. One of the female vocalists took the lead.

"No more crying!" she sang. "Denise is going to see her King!"

Twenty seconds into the song Deandra let out another loud wail.

Jeff put his arms around his daughter, wishing he could ease her pain. He wished it were him lying in the casket and not Denise. He'd trade places with his ex-wife in a heartbeat. She didn't deserve this. She had so much to live for. He closed his eyes, admitting to himself that he wasn't ready to let her go.

Hallelujah...Hallelujah...we're going to see the King!

The choir director then slowly put his hands down. The choir came to a low hum before he signaled them to take their seats.

Reverend Miles stepped up to the lectern and adjusted the microphone. "Friends and family, we are here today to celebrate the homegoing of Denise Elaine Jackson. She will be well missed, but do know that this is not a 'goodbye.' It's an 'until we meet again.' Denise was a fine young woman and she accomplished many great things. But we have to remember that she was only on loan to us."

Grace sobbed into her tissue as the reverend's words sent chills through her body. "My baby," she mumbled.

Nadine couldn't stop the tears from streaming down her face. Jeff handed her his handkerchief. Hearing Deandra's and Grace's sobs only worsened his own. He was sorry for everything that had happened before Denise's accident, feeling as though he were somehow to blame for her death.

The pastor spoke powerful words that had the entire room shedding tears and agreeing with his comforting words. He then read a scripture from the Old Testament.

Nadine sat motionless, her body feeling as though it were going into shock as she stared at Denise's obituary. A collage of colorful memories filled the second page. Some were photos of Denise as a child and a few when she was in college. Nadine had been included in several of the pictures. She remembered one picture vividly, with Denise and her sorors. It was the day they both pledged Delta Sigma Theta. Her eyes scrolled to another memory of her best friend. It was a picture of them cutting the ribbon at their first Platinum Crest Investments gala. Nadine's eyelids hurt so badly she couldn't bear to open them completely. As she read through tributes from both family and friends, the more Denise's death started to sink in. Denise wasn't coming back. She was gone. A big bulge of guilt worked Nadine over. What had she done? She kept asking herself the question, feeling as though somehow, someway, Denise's death could have been prevented.

Reverend Miles took his seat after the brief sermon. Sister Betty took that as her cue and limped slowly, using her cane and the assistance of one of the attendants, to the front of the church.

"I've known Denise since she was a young child," she began. "I watched her grow up and become a woman that made her mother so proud. I remember when Grace bought Denise her first car." She smiled at the memory. "She couldn't drive it to save her life, but she told Grace she would teach herself how to drive. And you better believe she did. See Denise was a stubborn old thing." Sister Betty looked at Grace, her longtime friend, for corroboration. Grace nodded.

The interplay brought a temporary smile to some of the faces that had been flushed with tears.

"Denise had the biggest heart," Sister Betty went on. "And what I would hope you will remember is the way she touched each of our lives. She may be gone, but not forgotten." With that Sister Betty was helped back to her seat while the next scheduled speaker came up.

Tonya sniffed a little before she began. "It seems like it was just yesterday that we were laughing and talking, at work, over left-over pizza," she said, managing a soft chuckle. "Denise was a terrific person. She was so young and full of life. I'm definitely going to miss her..." Her voice trailed off. She couldn't continue.

Reverend Miles stood and walked over to the lectern. "If anyone else has any remarks, please come up now."

Grace rocked Deandra in her arms, then unfolded the sheet of paper that Deandra had given her earlier that morning. She handed the paper to her granddaughter, wiped the corners of Deandra's eyes.

Jeff and Nadine both watched as Deandra walked to the front, near her mother's casket, and stood center. She held the piece of paper in her hands and began to read the poem she had written for her mom.

An angel came to me in my dream last night. She told me to dry my eyes and then she touched my heart with the big bright light. She told me she would follow me everywhere I go and make sure that I'm all right. Then she kissed my forehead and disappeared into the night. My Mommy is gone but she's still here with me, because the light she gave me, I locked it inside of my heart real tight.

Tears rolled down Deandra's face as she walked back to her seat. There wasn't a dry eye in the room but it was time for the viewing of the body. The pallbearers removed the bouquet of ivory, yellow, and purple flowers that rested on top of Denise's casket.

Nadine felt the stirrings of another asthma attack so she took two puffs of her pump to try and avoid it.

"Are you all right?" Jeff asked.

"Yes," Nadine replied with a tremble in her voice.

Reverend Miles stepped away from the lectern as the pallbearers stood to their feet.

Sister Michelle started the CD player and the soulful gospel singer Mahalia Jackson's "Nobody Knows the Trouble I've Seen" filled the church. One of the pallbearers opened the casket.

Denise looked so peaceful. Almost as if she was only sleeping. She was dressed in an ivory dress with pearls around her neck and in her ears. Her hair was styled in short silky curls and the right side was pinned back with her mother's pearl hairpin. When the pallbearer stepped aside, the clear visual of Denise lay before them. An outpour of cries came from the front row, Deandra screaming and shaking, Jeff leaning into her as she buried her face in his chest.

"Why'd you leave me, chile?" Grace cried out to her daughter.

Tonya rubbed Grace's back, trying to console her.

Jeff held his daughter tightly, barely able to look at Denise's lifeless body. He didn't want to see her like that. He looked up to the ceiling, telling God that He had made a mistake. Telling Him 'You should have taken me instead.'

Nadine's chest felt so tight that she could barely breathe. She had cried so much that she didn't think she had any tears left, but the tears streaming from her eyes now had proven that thought wrong. She fanned herself with the obituary, pacing her breathing.

The attendants had everyone on the back row stand. They motioned for them to move to the right and come down the side so that they could view the body.

Greg followed the lead of the others in front of him. He had felt extremely bad about the argument he and Denise had just before she died. Now, he was there to pay his respects and say his peace. As he walked past the front pew, he recognized Nadine. He turned his head quickly, hoping that she wouldn't notice him. With every step he took, bringing him closer to his ex lover's dead body, a deeper guilt rose within his chest. Greg stared down at Denise's body, said his peace, and then walked back to his seat.

Once everyone had gone up, the ushers rolled the casket closer to the front bench where Denise's immediate family sat.

Deandra brought her head up from her father's sleeve and let out a loud scream when she saw her mother. "Mommy, please don't leave me!" she cried.

"Come back," Jeff kept saying. "Please come back." He couldn't bear the pain building in his chest.

As Mahalia's voice came to an end, the choir rose from their seats. Although the members had been crying, they knew it was a celebration. One of their male singers led them through the words of "Here I Am" by Marvin Sapp.

Nadine placed her hand on top of her friend, an indescribable feeling coursing through her body. She leaned over and hugged Denise's cold casket. "I'm sorry," she said over and over, seemingly taking Denise's death the hardest. She stomped her feet. "Why!"

Fifteen more minutes of mourning and Denise's casket was closed. The six pallbearers all stood from their seats and walked over to the casket. They lifted it into the air and carried it out of the building.

The ushers directed the family members sitting in the front to stand and led them outside of the church and back to their limo and town cars. A sea of grieving faces followed as they all headed to the cemetery to put Denise in her final resting place.

31

*J*eff and Nadine rode in silence the entire way to the burial site. The limo their chauffer was following pulled into the gated cemetery and parked in a designated spot.

Nadine looked at Jeff through watery eyes as their Town Car came to a stop. She wondered what was going through his mind. When the driver opened her door, she exited to the left and Jeff moved out to the right. She waited for him to come to her side before walking ahead. His eyes finally met hers and she smiled at him. "We'll get through this together," she said.

Jeff just nodded his head, his mind spinning out of control.

Greg parked his car and followed in the direction everyone else was headed. He hadn't planned on going to the cemetery but decided at the last minute to pay his final respects as Denise was laid to rest. It was a beautiful day outside and as he removed his shades from his red and swollen eyes, the sun beamed down on his face. He took a spot next to Joseph Humphrey, who had also gone to pay his respects and give his condolences. The old and wealthy white man paid for the full cost of the funeral and the dinner taking place later at Denise's mother's house.

"How you holding up, man?" Mr. Humphrey asked Greg.

Greg shook his head. "I'm still coming down from all of it," he admitted, still shocked by it all. "How's the Missus?"

"Fine," Joseph said. "My wife wanted to come but she doesn't handle funerals very well."

"Mine either," Greg said, watching the family make room under the green tent.

Joseph turned to him. "So did Vivian ever find out about the two of you?" he asked in a hushed tone.

Greg twisted his face. "What are you talking about, man?" he asked, staring straight ahead.

"You know good and damn well what I'm talking about, so don't bullshit with me," Joseph said.

They both went quiet.

"Vivian knows that I love her and that she has nothing to worry about," Greg said, sounding so self-assured.

"Really?" Joseph chuckled, revealing his perfectly straight, white, porcelain veneers.

"What's all that for?" Greg questioned as he turned back to face Joseph.

"Nothing at all. This old man doesn't know anything," Joseph stated with a straight face.

Greg's brows furrowed as he watched the small huddle around the grave get bigger. Directly across from him under the tent sat Denise's grieving family, including the woman who had beaten him across the back with an umbrella the day he was caught having sex with Denise at her office. The woman was blotting the tears from her eyes, never taking her eyes off of the casket.

"If you'll please bow your head for prayer," Reverend Miles said. He lowered his own head. "We brought nothing into this world, and it is certain we can carry nothing out. The Lord gave, and the Lord hath taken away. Denise will be truly missed but in no way will she ever be forgotten. She's a child of our Father and He has asked that she return home."

Cries erupted throughout the crowd.

The reverend finished his prayer, then lifted his head. The pall-bearers walked over to the casket and placed it on the green straps. They secured it and proceeded to lower her body into the ground.

"We commend unto Thy hands of mercy, most merciful Father, the soul of our sister departed, and we commit her body to the ground. Earth to earth, ashes to ashes, dust to dust; and we beseech Thine infinite goodness to give us grace to live in Thy fear and love and to die in Thy favour, that when the judgment shall come which Thou hast committed to Thy well-beloved Son, both our sister and we may be found acceptable in Thy sight. O merciful Father, for the sake of Jesus Christ, our only Saviour, we send her home."

A few people stood and dropped single flowers into the ground. Grace couldn't move. She stayed in her seat while Deandra dropped flower petals over her mother's grave. Once done she took a seat beside Grace again.

"What is *he* doing here?" Nadine said a little louder than intended once she looked up and saw Greg.

Jeff followed Nadine's eyes. "Who is he?" he asked casually.

Without thinking, she answered, "He's a *special* Platinum Crest Investments client. His name is Greg Adams."

Jeff's face scrunched all on its own. Why in the hell did that name sound familiar? He thought about the hotel receipts he had found in one of Denise's old purses and the cell phone statement that had come in the mail last month. Then suddenly Greg in his tailored suit, polished shoes, and platinum cufflinks was heading in his direction.

Greg moved through the assembly and walked over to where

Grace, Nadine, and Denise's ex-husband were still seated. He walked straight to Grace. "I'm sorry about your loss, ma'am. Your daughter was a very special friend of mine."

Jeff looked down at the man's wrist where a black and gold Rolex embedded in canary yellow diamonds laid comfortably.

Greg moved down the row and when he extended his hand to shake Nadine's, Jeff slapped it away. "Don't touch her, mother-fucker!"

Everybody looked in Jeff's direction, baffled at what was happening. Tonya lifted her shades and covered her mouth in pure shock as she began to put two and two together.

Greg drew his neck back and lifted his hands. He backed away. "I was just offering—"

"We don't need shit from you! You've done enough for my family," Jeff snapped, each word dripping with malice. Jeff had a permanent hate for Greg and the frightening part about it was that the rage coursing through his veins was unpredictable. So the longer Greg stood there, the more his life was in jeopardy.

All eyes were fixated on Greg and Jeff. Grace brought herself to her feet. She stepped in between them. "You are not going to do this *here!*" she said with her finger pointed to the ground as tears continued to roll down her face.

"I apologize," Greg said sympathetically, his eyes still on Jeff. "I'll be leaving now."

Jeff and Nadine watched Greg walk away. When Nadine reached to hold Jeff's hand, he jerked away, turning cold on her. "What's wrong?" she asked, clearly hurt.

Jeff shook his head at her but his eyes revealed his every thought. Realizing how she had known about Greg just like she had known about Deandra not being his child, made his stomach knot. He stared her down as though she were a complete stranger. "I'll be in the car." With those last words hanging in the air, he got up from his seat and started to walk off.

"Jeff. Wait," Nadine called out. She ignored the stares the commotion had drawn and walked quickly to catch up to him. She called out his name as she followed him, only for her calls to fall on deaf ears. She passed their chauffeur who asked if they were ready to leave. "Give us a few minutes, please," she told him.

Jeff opened the car door, got in the backseat, and tried to calm down all on his own. His heart was racing just as fast as his thoughts. Before he knew it, his mind started to play tricks on him. Nadine didn't love him, he told himself. As far as he was concerned, their relationship had been all a game. It was clear to him now.

Nadine climbed inside the car. The cool air brought her immediate relief. "What happened back there?" she asked, catching her breath.

Jeff didn't answer her.

She paused for a moment. "So is this how we're going to get through this?" she asked, confused.

Jeff finally brought his eyes to hers. "What else are you keeping from me, huh?"

Nadine allowed Jeff's words to register. Before she knew it, karma had found its way back into her life. It had hunted her down like a bounty hunter on a million dollar mission and she had nowhere to run. Nowhere to hide. Even her aunt had warned her of this. "Baby, I'm sorry," she mumbled.

Jeff let out a loose chuckle. Suddenly this shit was beginning to feel like déjà vu all over again. "What exactly are you sorry for, Nadine? The fact that you've been keeping shit from me since day one?"

Nadine pressed her lips together, seemingly at a loss for words. But the true reason for her silence was that of guilt and shame.

She had betrayed him and there was nothing she could say or do to change that brutal reality. So why even bother trying? Jeff would never understand because he would never take the time to hear her side of the story. See things her way. He would never see that she was only trying to protect his feelings.

"Tsk. I thought we had something. You damn sure fooled me."

Nadine's eyes found his. "We do."

Jeff's face begged to differ.

"We can fix this. I promise."

"Don't you get it? There's nothing to fix!" Jeff snapped.

"But I love you!" Nadine cried.

"Yeah. And I *thought* I loved you, too."

Minutes later their chauffer headed back to the vehicle. Oblivious to the heated exchange that took place just before, he offered a crying Nadine a box of Kleenex.

They rode in silence the rest of the way while Jeff contemplated his next move. This was the hand life had dealt him and no matter how fucked up it was, he still held all the cards. He questioned God for so many reasons, desperate for answers that didn't seem to exist. He was mentally exhausted but he still found himself thinking about Denise. He missed her so much and the burdening reminder that she was gone, weighed on him like a ton of bricks. He let his head fall back against the headrest. Tears began to well in his eyes but he quickly blinked them back. He wouldn't allow his body to surrender to the pain tearing him up from the inside. But that persistent twinge soon began rising in his chest, suffocating him. His once stable breathing fell to short gasps. Jeff was hurting. He was grieving. And for a long moment, he thought that he was dying.

32

One year later

Nadine was back at Platinum Crest Investments, working in her new office when Tonya stuck her head in the door. "You have a visitor," Tonya said, smiling as she rubbed her protruding belly.

"Who is it?" Nadine asked, engulfed in all the work she had before her. Ever since the audit from SEC, she'd been on pins and needles trying to turn the place around. She had Jim, her new partner, assisting her with everything Denise left behind. Turned out that Denise had been forging financial statements and falsifying legal documents for her clients, placing their business in a whirlwind of trouble.

"They asked me not to say," Tonya said.

Nadine looked at Tonya suspiciously and then rolled her eyes playfully. "Send them in."

A few seconds later, in walked Jeff, holding baby Canvas.

Nadine got up from her leather recliner and hurried over to them. She held out her hands and Canvas reached for her. "Hey, Mama's big boy," she sang and cooed.

"What about me?" Jeff asked. "Daddy wants some sugar, too."

Nadine smiled, then leaned in and gave Jeff a kiss on the cheek. While she realized that they had an agreement to remain close friends, Nadine would be lying if she said that she didn't still have feelings for her child's father. But she respected his wishes and gave him his space. The only time they saw each other was when he and Deandra would drop Canvas off from daycare.

Nadine hadn't been with anyone since Jeff and she didn't even have the desire for another man. She wanted Jeff and if she couldn't have the man of her dreams, the love of her life, then she would stay single. She was convinced that there was no one else out there for her.

"Well, Canvas and I thought you might be hungry so we wanted to take you out for lunch."

"Aww...how thoughtful." Nadine smiled brightly. She was not going to turn down food. She grabbed her coat off of the coat rack. "Where are we going?"

"Your choice," Jeff said.

With her chunky and healthy child hanging off her left hip, Nadine turned off her computer monitor. "My choice, huh. Hmm...Cheesecake Factory."

"Sounds like a winner to me." Jeff opened the door wider so that she and Canvas could pass through. When she brushed past him he grabbed her gently by the elbow.

Nadine just looked at him. His eyes saying all of the things his mouth had yet to say. She read his face.

"I miss you so much," Jeff admitted.

Nadine turned completely around to face him. "I've missed you, too."

Jeff took a deep breath. He looked at his son who was a spitting image of him. Not only did Jeff know that Canvas was his based on looks alone, but Nadine had bought an over the counter DNA kit, to reassure Jeff. She didn't want him to ever have any doubts about their son.

"Nadine, we've been through a lot," Jeff started. "But I'm ready to be there for you and our son, the way a real man should." He paused. "I never stopped loving you," he confessed.

Nadine's eyes couldn't help but water. She had waited so long to hear this.

"I can't live another day, another hour, or another minute, knowing that I might wake up one day with regrets." With that, Jeff positioned himself on one knee. He pulled out the silver square box that held the platinum two-karat diamond ring he had purchased weeks before.

Nadine pressed her trembling lips together.

"Baby, I'm tired of being lonely," Jeff said, smiling up at Nadine.

Nadine's heart pumped faster and faster as chills ran up and down her spine.

"So will you please do me the honor of being my wife?"

Nadine tried to formulate a sentence but couldn't. Instead she nodded her head repeatedly, until the words finally made their way out. "Yes! Yes! I'll marry you."

Jeff slipped the ring on her left finger and then rushed her with a kiss so passionate, baby Canvas covered his eyes. Suddenly everyone in Platinum Crest that had witnessed Jeff's proposal started clapping. Including clients.

"A new beginning," Jeff said to his future wife.

Smiling, Nadine repeated those exact words as she placed her hand in his and started for the door.

ABOUT THE AUTHOR

N'Tyse is a Dallas, Texas native and bestselling author of *Twisted Seduction*. While N'Tyse, pronounced "entice," spells out exotic seduction, the true significance behind her name takes on an entire new meaning. **N**ever **T**ell **Y**our **S**ecrets is the hidden message N'Tyse envelops within her stimulating taboo tales.

N'Tyse's writing career began at a very young age where she found poetry, music, and story-telling as an outlet of escape. Now 30, the writer's obsession with the pen is better described as the "intimate release" for her imagination. In 2007, she ambitiously penned and self-published her freshman novel, *My Secrets Your Lies*. Upon the release of her first book, she discovered that her hobby-writing was no longer just a niche to satisfy that writing craving, but a true talent where her underlying passion awaited. In late October 2010, N'Tyse acquired a literary agent and soon landed her first major publishing deal with Strebor Books/Simon & Schuster.

N'Tyse currently juggles her writing career as a mom, wife, and full-time personal banker, while also pursuing her bachelor's degree in creative/film writing and business entertainment. Her latest works include *Stud Princess Notorious Vendettas*. Her features include *Missionary No More: Purple Panties 2, Bedtime Stories, Between the Sheets, Erotic Snapshots, Gutta Mamis*, and *Chocolate Flava 3*. N'Tyse is currently hard at work on her upcoming novel, *Staged*, and documentary film, *Beneath My Skin*.

For more updates, go beyond the pages and satisfy your curiosity:
www.ntyse.com
www.facebook.com/author.ntyse
www.twitter.com/ntyse
www.myspace.com/ntyse
ntyse.amillionthoughts@yahoo.com

IF YOU LIKED N'TYSE'S "TWISTED SEDUCTION," WE HOPE YOU'LL TRY ANOTHER AUTHOR IN THE STREBOR FAMILY. BE SURE TO CHECK OUT

At The End Of The Day

BY SUZETTA PERKINS
AVAILABLE MAY 2012 FROM STREBOR BOOKS

ENJOY THIS SNEAK PREVIEW!

1

Rain threatened the New York sky. Rain or shine, there was going to be a wedding. It had been postponed six months because Denise Thomas wanted to share her special day close to her family and in the city of her birth rather than in Birmingham, Alabama, where she now lived with her fiancé, Harold, and their daughter, eight-year-old Danica. New York in December would not lend itself to the fabulous venue she'd chosen for her nuptials; however, on this June day that still held promise, she was going to marry her lover, the man she adored, and the cousin of her ex-husband.

Denise sat in the white Rolls-Royce limousine with its spacious, luxury interior flanked by her mother, grandmother, daughter, and two sisters. She watched as her guests arrived dressed in their finest although it was the middle of the day, taking in the splendor of the crabapple trees, the beautiful violet flowers, and the rest of the floral extravagance that comprised Central Park in the Conservatory Garden. Conservatory Garden was said to be one of the hidden wonders of Central Park and a favorite place to have a wedding.

And then she saw them, Sylvia and Kenny Richmond—Sylvia dressed in an emerald green lightweight wool and silk skirt-suit with faux-jewel buttons; Rachel and Marvin Thomas—Rachel dressed in a stunning red Italian wool crepe suit that boasted a stand up-collar on her raglan-sleeve jacket over a matching classic skirt; Claudette and Tyrone Beasley—Claudette dressed in a Caroline Rose mushroom-colored long jacket of Italian polyester with an oversized collar and a matching scoop-neck tank and black silk slacks; Trina and Cecil Coleman—Trina in an ultra conservative charcoal skirt-suit with a classic V-neck collar and embroidered front panel; and the ever classy Mona and Michael Broussard—Mona dressed in an Albert Nipon onyx polyester and wool skirt-suit that looked absolutely fabulous on her. They were her special family, and they strolled in the garden like they were New York elitists, each lady's arm seductively looped in the arm of her husband. They blended well with the movers and shakers that were New York. It was Harold's family that brought the 'Bama with them, however, it didn't matter to Denise because this was her day.

Everything was planned down to the minute. The ceremony was to take no more than forty-five minutes, according to Denise's wedding planner. Then it would be on to the Roosevelt Hotel for the fabulous reception that would rival any platinum wedding that was showcased on television.

It was time. At the direction of the wedding planner, the bridal party was ushered from the limousine to the elaborate makeshift staging area to await their cues. Denise could hear the beautiful melodies of the string violinists floating in the air and could feel the anticipation of the guests as they waited for her to come down the aisle. Her mother and grandmother were escorted to their seats. Her sisters, who served as maid of honor and bridesmaid, respectively, glided down the aisle, each in knee-length, strapless lavender satin dresses and diamond lily brooches that served as hair accents placed in half-moon clusters in their upswept hair. With long, Shirley Temple curls that hung past her shoulders, Danica dressed in a beautiful white satin cream dress with ruffles at the bottom waited to walk in before Denise so she could sprinkle lavender rose petals on the ground.

And then they were playing her music. All eyes were on Denise as she floated down the aisle as if walking on air, savoring every minute and in perfect time with the musicians. Her bronze-colored skin was radiant in a sleek satin organza strapless gown that conformed to her body, accentuating her curves like a fine piece of sculpture. The sweetheart neckline wrapped in a beaded overlay draped her shapely breast and her manufactured one like a freshwater mermaid, while the satin skirt was embellished with a beaded lace overlay accentuated with freshwater pearls, Swarovski crystals and rhinestones with sleek satin-covered buttons that ran the length of the entire back of the gown. A ten-carat diamond Eternity necklace decorated Denise's neck. Setting it all off was a bouquet of lavender roses mixed with sweet peas and parrot tulips that Denise clutched tightly in her hand.

Denise's thin lips stretched into an elongated smile when she finally looked ahead and saw Harold waiting for her and Danica standing beside her aunt holding the satin basket that was full of rose petals only moments before. Denise was the happiest she'd be in a long time.

"I pronounce you man and wife," the minister finally said, clad in his black and purple ministerial robe after a twenty minute heartfelt ceremony that had guests dabbing at their eyes two or three times. "You may now kiss the bride."

Harold held his bride and kissed her passionately, Denise not shy in reciprocating. Loud claps erupted from the two-hundred guests who gave their approval of what they had witnessed. And when Harold and Denise finally parted their lips, the clapping intensified, sounding like thunder. The bride and groom turned to the audience, Denise waiving her hand for all to see. They jumped the broom, the fairly new tradition in African-American wedding ceremonies, and walked up the aisle arm in arm ready to start their brand new life together. As if on cue, the sun peaked and immersed itself fully from behind the cloud that had threatened rain all morning, lighting up the New York sky in a blaze of glory.

"Denise is absolutely gorgeous," Sylvia said, as she and Kenny along with the other four couples filed out behind the wedding party to offer congratulations to the new bride and groom.

"Denise? Shoot, this place is fabulous," Mona said, still gazing at the floral splendor that made the Conservatory so popular among prospective brides. "Yeah, Denise looks pretty, too. Doesn't she, Marvin?"

"Okay, Mona, no need to press Marvin's buttons," Michael said, giving his wife a tiny jab in the ribs.

"It's okay," Marvin said. "Yes, Denise is beautiful and she looks happy, too. See, my boo," he winked at Rachel, "knows that I love her and only her."

"Mona, you did comprehend what my boo said?" Rachel countered, flicking her hand in Mona's direction. "Now shut up and let's get through this and enjoy the rest of the festivities. We know that Denise is going to show out because she wants us southerners to know how they do it in the Big Apple. That's why she didn't want to get married in Birmingham."

"Hmmph, I think we look better than the rest of her guests," Claudette chimed in. "Maybe Denise doesn't realize that Atlanta is right next to New York when it comes to bourgeoisie."

Everyone laughed.

"You tell them, Claudette," Mona said, trying to quiet the laughter.

"Well, New York has a flare of its own that trumps Atlanta, L.A...." Trina began. Sylvia, Mona, Rachel, and Claudette threw their hands on their hips and twisted their bodies to look Trina in the eyes.

"Says who?" Mona huffed. "I'm from New Orleans, and I know we have a zest for the flare, but since I claim Atlanta as home, I'm here to tell you that it rivals all those big cities you named. Why else would everyone want to move there? You can't tell me that we don't entertain, that we don't live in fabulous houses, have as much disposable income, and can rock fashion right along with these wannabe New York socialites. Look at me. I catered an event for then Senator Barack Obama, who is now the forty-fourth president of the United States. What black socialite in New York can say they've done that?"

"All right, you've made your point," Trina said. "It's that…"

"It's that…nothing," Mona said, cutting Trina off. "I can compete with anybody, no matter where they come from…Los Angeles, Milan, Paris, and New York."

Trina rolled her eyes at Mona, while the others stifled a laugh.

"Okay, ladies, this is Denise and Harold's day," Sylvia said. "She wanted to have her wedding in New York so she would be close to her family. That's all."

"Yeah, right," Mona said, pulling her lipstick out of her purse and dabbing a little on her lips.

"I'm not in it," Kenny said, as Cecil glanced in his direction.

"Me either," Tyrone offered.

"You all know my wife," Michael uttered. "She can't keep her mouth closed and it's always going to flap a mile a minute. Mona didn't mean any harm, Trina."

Trina smirked but changed it to a smile as they approached the newlyweds.

Trina gave Denise an air kiss to each cheek. "You are so beautiful, Denise. God smiled on you today."

"Thanks, Trina. I feel wonderful—got my soul mate and our daughter standing next to me. Look at this rock?" Denise stuck her manicured hand out for Trina to see.

"It's beautiful."

"Five carats, Trina." Denise smiled. "I'm glad you and Cecil could come."

"We wouldn't have missed it for anything in the world."

"Move the line along," Mona called out.

"Wait your turn," Trina shot back.

"Girl, Mona isn't going to change," Denise said to Trina.

"Tell me about it."

Cecil kissed Denise, and he and Trina shook hands with Harold and the rest of the party.

"Look at my girls," Denise said as Mona, Rachel, Sylvia and Claudette surrounded her, leaving their husbands to stand behind them. "You all look fabulous...came to show these New Yorkers a thing or two."

"What did I say?" Mona put in, although Sylvia, Rachel, and Claudette ignored her.

"You are a beautiful bride," Sylvia said as she kissed Denise on the cheek.

"Ditto," Rachel said, taking her turn to give Denise a kiss.

"I've got to give it to you, Denise," Mona said. "You did it like I would have done it. I think both of us would've looked fabulous in that dress, and when you walked down the aisle, you worked it girl...wanted everyone to know that you were the exclusive...the headline news at eleven. I'm glad the rain decided to hold off."

"Well, thank you, Mona. I'll take that as a compliment from you. But I'm so glad you are all here to share in my day. I remember each of your weddings as if they happened yesterday. Why are you being so quiet, Claudette? Give me a hug."

"I wasn't being quiet although no one can get anything in edgewise with Mrs. Mona Broussard flapping her chops," Claudette said. Everyone laughed. "But you look so beautiful today, Denise. I was thinking that maybe T and I will renew our vows one day and have a big shindig. I can afford it now."

"Yeah, I heard you have a world-class stylin' salon up in one of those fancy buildings in Atlanta with clientele that boasts many of Atlanta's rich and famous."

"She and T are also rocking in a brand new home that none of us have seen yet," Mona said, cutting in.

"So you've heard about me?" Claudette said with a smile on her face. She was surprised to know that Denise had knowledge of her success.

"Claudette, I would've had you do my hair if I was getting married in Birmingham. I love you all." Denise hesitated. "Are you going to give me a hug, Marvin?"

Marvin smiled as Rachel looked on. He placed a kiss on Denise's cheek and shook Harold's hand. "You both look wonderful and happy," Marvin said, not addressing his comment to only Denise.

Denise wondered how Marvin really felt seeing her and Harold together as husband and wife. She missed Marvin in many ways. He was so caring and loving. He'd do anything for her. Maybe if Marvin hadn't been so married to his job, they'd still be married, although it was her selfishness, if she was grown enough to admit it, which pulled her away from him. Then again and truth be told, it was her blatant indiscretion, her infidelity, her being caught with Marvin's cousin, the man who was now her husband, in a compromising position that broke the camel's back. The only thing Marvin was guilty of was planting the seed for what was now a giant Fortune 500 corporation for which Rachel now received the benefits. She wasn't mad because in the end, Denise knew that Harold was where her heart truly belonged.